MW00941490

THE RESISTANCE

THE UNCLOAKED TRILOGY BOOK ONE

J. RODES

WORDS THAT EDIFY

Rooted Publishing

THE RESISTANCE

Copyright © 2017 by Jennifer Rodewald.

This book is a work of fiction. Names, characters, businesses, organizations, places, events and incidents either are the product of the author's imagination or are used fictitiously. Any resemblance to actual persons, living or dead, events, or locales is entirely coincidental.

For information contact :

http://www.authorjenrodewald.com

Cover design by Roseanna White @ RoseannaWhiteDesigns.com

Images from Shutterstock.com and Lightstock.com

Party Seal by Kailynn Rodewald

ISBN: 978-1-7268774-2-8

Published by Rooted Publishing

McCook, NE 69001

First Edition: April 2017

❀ Created with Vellum

Will you stand?

CHAPTER ONE

"THEY'VE WON. GOD HELP US."

I glanced toward my father, who spoke near the television. His eyes moved with meticulous intent, connecting with each solemn face in the multipurpose room of our church. You'd have thought he was conducting a funeral, with the way concern engraved his lined expression.

"We need to pray." He slid from his seat to his knees. "Now."

Every last one of the twenty-six people who had gathered to watch the election results followed his lead. Crikey. Like it was the end of the world. How many elections had been held in this country? Established almost three hundred years before, the States weren't going to fold because one bad apple rode a Progressive Reform ticket into the White House.

Drama. That was what this was all about. Father was all about finding ways to motivate his flock.

Apathy is the illness of the overprivileged Christian. That had been the theme of his last sermon, given on Sunday as a last-ditch attempt to get people into the voting machines. I glanced around the room. Twenty-six people. Out of a congregation of nearly five hundred, only twenty-six showed up to watch the results and to pray. I'd say Father's attempt failed.

People understood more than Father thought. Maybe more than he understood himself. Kasen Asend would take office in January, twiddle around the White House for four years, and if he was lucky—and careful to remain in the public's good graces—he'd rack up another four years. That was it. Eight years, and he'd be confined to the history books that nobody ever read. What kind of ghastly imprint could he really leave in only eight years?

Nothing worth all this bizarre fear.

I pretended to bow in prayer. "Come on." Leaning into Eliza Knight, I whispered near her ear. "Let's go. The youth room's empty."

"Shhh." She shrugged me away.

I leaned in closer. "We can play foosball. I'll let you win."

Raising her head, she shot me a scowl. "I think we should pray."

"They've got it covered." I tugged on her elbow.

Her shoulders slumped. I hated when she was disappointed. But I couldn't stand being there, and somewhere in her pious little head, she couldn't either. There was no way she could. Of all the people in our congregation, the Knights were the most faithful, which meant Eliza and her little sister, Hannah, were stuck at church almost as much as I was. Board meetings. Sunday dinners. Choir rehearsal. Wednesday night Bible club. Thursday night Bible study. Our whole lives revolved around the doings of this church. It got old.

I rose from my knees, my hand still gripping her elbow. Eliza hesitated, but I knew she wouldn't resist me. I was right. Eliza wasn't a fighter. She hated conflict. I rather delighted in a good clash—not with her, but with just about anyone else. I'd fight before I'd bend.

We slipped out the door, and I was careful to hold the handle so the latch wouldn't click. When you grew up in the middle of meetings and meetings and more meetings, you learned how to be sneaky. I had it down to a science. Eliza would have too, if she'd have ever put her mind to it.

"What'd you do that for?" she hissed after I secured the door.

"What do you mean?"

"We're in trouble." Panic painted her eyes with fear.

I smirked, shaking my head. "We never get caught. They don't care anyway. None of that's about you or me."

"Our *country* is in trouble, Braxton." She swallowed loud enough for me to hear. "More so than even during the Bloody Faith Conflict. We should be in there praying. It will affect all of us."

Rolling my eyes, I took her arm again and marched down the hall toward the youth room. "You've been listening to our fathers too much. Don't panic. It's just an election, same as the one four years ago, same as it will be in another four years. Stop getting caught in all the freaking hype."

She freed her elbow and grabbed my hand, yanking me to a stop. "It's not hype. Don't you understand what the Progressive creed means? *By our hands*. It's defiance. Rebellion against everything that has allowed the US to be successful in the first place. Do you think God will continue to protect a nation that has brazenly rejected Him?"

I huffed. "Stop quoting my father's sermons. I hear them all week. And it is hype. Panic. You're smarter than that, Eliza."

Actually, I didn't think God cared one way or the other

how our country voted. He hadn't been too involved in the conflict that had ripped apart our nation twenty-five years before, and since our once megachurch was turning into something more like a minichurch, it didn't look like He had much interest in that either. And either way, it didn't matter. I had a life to carve out, no matter what the government or my father's church did.

"What if he's right?" Eliza leaned in close enough that I could smell her strawberry gum. "What if Kasen Asend's hatred of the church—of God—leads to persecution? What will we do?"

"My father *isn't* right." I squeezed her hand and turned back toward the youth room. "You'll see. It's just an emotional fool's reaction because we didn't get our way. Trust me. By the time we graduate and move off to college, we'll be laughing at the way everyone got all stirred up about it. Nothing bad is going to happen."

I really believed it. Turned out, I was the fool.

CHAPTER TWO

SCHOOL WAS ALIVE THE NEXT DAY. BUZZING ABOUT progress, or change at last, or all the free stuff the turnover election would introduce. President-elect Kasen Asend had made all sorts of promises. Free healthcare for every citizen of the US. Equalized standards of living throughout the country. Citizenship for those who had been denied, or for those whose families had been deported during the eastern scare, because he would redefine what citizenship required. *A nation transformed.* That had been his platform.

That was the mantra of the day.

The upperclassmen had gone full-fledged crazy during the election. I wasn't sure what had them so stirred up. Perhaps the same overblown plug that had my father and Eliza riled. Whatever it was, the seniors especially had gone stupid-insane over the political turnover. A huge majority of them showed up wearing T-shirts boasting the Progressive Party's logo—a fist clutching a sledgehammer with their creed printed in an arc. *By our hands.*

I had to admit, that made even me cringe.

I wasn't the humblest of guys, but I could recognize outright arrogance printed on a T-shirt. But still, I figured it'd blow over. Presidents came and went. Made a whole lot of windy promises, only to leave the White House with a mediocre record at best. Most were lucky to keep even one of their farfetched pledges. Kasen had a whole book made out. He wouldn't even make the ticket next election. He'd shot himself dead in the water for the next round of votes because he'd made so many rainbow promises.

Hype. Everywhere I went, hype. What was with all these people? Give it a week. It'd all settle like the chalk rock on the football field after a collision. I ignored the image of the field after the game—smudged lines and smeared end zones. That wasn't prophetic. Couldn't be.

I cut a wake through the sea of propaganda T-shirts and met Eliza by her locker. A bluish tinge colored the skin under her eyes, but she attempted a smile when she looked up at me.

"Tired?" I spun so that I could lean against the locker next to hers while she scanned the lock with her code-card.

She nodded while slipping her text-tablet under her arm, and then she flashed her code-card over the scanner so the locker would close again.

"Why?" I asked as pushed off the lockers. "The prayer meeting ended before midnight this time. We've gone way later."

We walked down the hall toward her first math class. Last year, the end of our freshman school term, she'd tested into the premed Career Track, so her schedule had been loaded with math and science. I had tried to test into the engineering track. Failed by two questions. Typical Braxtonian luck. My older brothers couldn't fail at anything. I failed at everything. School, football, good looks—Jamis and Annyon swam in the deep waters of Luther success. I was stuck playing in the kiddie pool of mediocrity.

Good thing Eliza didn't seem to mind.

"Couldn't sleep last night," Eliza said, hugging her tab close to her stomach.

I rehashed the previous minutes in my head to remember what I'd asked her. Common for me. I was always getting sucked inside of myself like I was some kind of vortex of egocentric mania. I stopped, tugging on Eliza's shoulder so that she'd look at me. So that I could concentrate on her and not my inner ego. Or was it id? I was never going to pass psychology.

I bent a bit, tilting my neck so that I could have a good look at her walnut-brown eyes. She was more than tired. Fear lurked there.

"Liza, you're not still stewing about the election, are you?"

"Look around, Braxton." She glanced over one shoulder and then another. "Have you ever seen a student body this captivated? Kasen's charm has mesmerized the country. You can feel his presence even here, at school, where we usually don't care."

I scrunched my eyebrows. "And this makes you scared?"

Someone bumped Eliza from behind, tipping her toward me. I steadied her with a hand on her arm while at the same time looking for the klutz. I didn't have to search hard.

Garrison the Hulk sneered at her from behind. "Where's your patriotic spirit, Church Girl?"

The Progressive's logo stretched tight over his steroid-pumped pecs. Couldn't he find anything in a larger size? *T-shirts aren't made of spandex, buddy, and there's a reason.*

Eliza lifted her chin to see him. She held eye contact but didn't open her mouth. Déjà vu. One day two years ago, they'd been deadlocked like this on the bus ride home, back when

Garrison still rode the school bus. Eliza had spilled her soda on her school-issued tab and muttered *nuts* under her breath. Garrison laughed his bellowing *I mock you* laugh and dared her to say something saltier. He even offered a suggestion— something that Eliza would die before she ever allowed to escape from her lips. Garrison had egged her on in his obnoxious, *you must conform to me* way, while the rest of the kids on the bus sat muted to hear his challenge.

She'd met his eyes, and with a calm sternness that surprised everyone, including me, she said, "No."

That was it. They'd stared in icy gridlock until Garrison cracked another mocking snort. "Church girl," he'd hollered.

I had wished she would stand up for herself. She'd just held him with her gaze. Though I was only an eighth grader at the time, I had deemed it unacceptable.

"Does it make you feel like a big man to pick on a fourteen-year-old girl?" I'd challenged the Hulk.

To this day, I wasn't sure what I'd been thinking. Even as a sophomore, Garrison had been ripped. I was pretty sure he started lifting when he was five, and steroids were most definitely added to his regimen long before high school. I didn't have the signature Luther build—broad shoulders, barrel chest, and powerful legs. Somehow my father's endowment of strength missed me, probably because I was an afterthought in the procreation planning process. I'd been left with only height, which stunk because my long legs and stretched-out torso made me look like a string bean.

"Aw, isn't that special." Garrison had attempted a doe-eyed look, which came off like a deformity on his ugly and massive face. "The PK and the church girl. Heaven musta had a plan."

"Why are you still riding the school bus, Hulk?" My

mouth always came unhinged before I thought words through. "Wouldn't they let you on the big-people transport?"

I had gone home with my nose rearranged that afternoon.

That last part of the flashback hit me a little too late. Standing in the school hall with my feet planted like I was ready to take a three-point stance, I pulled Eliza's arm until she stepped behind me. Two years hadn't helped the string-bean dilemma, nor had it cured me of my snappy lip.

"No wonder they still won't let you ride with the adults." I scowled, only slightly aware of Eliza tugging on my arm. "Maybe you should worry more about your animallike people skills and less about what Eliza's wearing."

Hulk's nostrils flared as he stepped into my halo of space. Crikey. Me and my uncorked mouth.

"*You'd* better be worried about what she wears—and does. Worried for the both of you."

I'm pretty sure he growled as he drew a breath.

"I hear your father's been preaching against the Party, telling people not to vote for Kasen. Better watch your back, PK. This is the breaking of a new age, and your kind is on the fringe of extinction."

He glared at me long enough for my hair to grow, standing so close I could smell the rank mixture of garlic and tobacco on his hot breath. Apparently toothbrushes didn't figure into his daily routine.

I kept my tongue locked down—miraculously—and Hulk moved on, pushing against my shoulder as he passed.

"See," Eliza muttered from behind me. "You're not getting the big picture, Braxton."

I spun, irritation stamping a rhythm in my veins. Had she missed that I'd just stuck up for her—again? She lifted her wide brown eyes to me, sweet innocence squashed by concern, and my anger sifted to the floor.

I could never stay mad at Eliza. She was the kind of girl you just had to protect, because she was so innocent and sincerely kind, and because you knew you'd never meet another human being like her on the planet. Smart and quiet, but funny in her quirky little way, Eliza had a way of making you want the world to be the Garden it was supposed to have been. Because that was where she belonged.

I drew in a lungful of air, stale with the smell of freshmen who still hadn't figured out that deodorant wasn't optional and who wore shoes without socks a few times too many. I'd let her have her rant. She'd feel better, and then we could finally get past all this drama.

"All right, Eliza. Tell me what's got you so worried."

She lifted a glance to me. "Did you know there's a rally on Friday night?"

"Like a pep rally?" Figured. Guys like Kasen Asend needed cheering. Ego-heads always required an adoring crowd.

She started moving again, walking in the direction of her first-hour class. "More than that. It's a pledge rally."

A pledge rally? What were we now, Girl Scouts? Sorority sisters? I walked with her, this time careful about my next words. "What are they pledging?"

"Their lives and undivided allegiance to the Party." Panic made her whisper sound harsh.

I snorted. "What does that mean?"

We reached her classroom, and she tilted her pleading face, silently begging me to understand. "I don't know. But there's talk of receiving a brand on their neck to seal the oath."

Aha. Eliza had Revelation in her head. Her grandmother, a

little nutty to begin with, was always preaching about the end times. Apparently the old fanatic had gotten into Eliza's head.

"You're jumping to conclusions, Liza." I shook my head, knowing I stared at her like she was a theatrical child, and also knowing she hated that. "It's all going to blow over."

She drew up straight, her full height putting her almost to my chin. "I'm not thinking what you think I'm thinking." Her eyes met mine, a smolder of irritation replacing the fear. "I've read my Bible, Braxton Luther, and I know what it says about the mark of the Beast. I'm not a doomsayer. I've also read those history books you don't bother with. The end of the world isn't the only time persecution can happen."

Pivoting, she walked to her seat without looking back. I didn't think anyone irritated her like I did. I'd never seen her upset with another person the way she could get with me. But it was always short lived, and we moved on. Which was what I did. I had—of all things—history class to get to.

Settling at my desk, I opened my text-tab and tapped the History icon while I waited for the monitor at the front of the room to flash on. Teachers were minimal in our school—it was cheaper to broadcast a mass lesson from the biggest high school in our state, which was over a hundred miles away. Only the Career Track classes had real-live humans to interact with, because they paid tuition. That meant we lower-IQ dummies had to do our best on our own, dealing with the inevitable jerk who goofed around during the simulcast, and the brainless girls in the back who always talked the entire hour. Three weeks of lecture, followed by a unit test, and the cycle started all over. That was supposed to educate the unlearnable masses who couldn't test into a Career Track or afford to pay the fees.

Chances of me making it to any kind of reputable university were slim. But it had been done. I was going to have to slide into those narrow odds, because I didn't want to serve fast food or sweep a high school gymnasium floor for the rest of my life.

The monitor at the front of the room lit up, and Mr. Nigel, our on-screen teacher, appeared wearing a Party T-shirt. "This is a great day in American history, class." He always started his lectures that way, but that day he seemed especially swayed by his assertion. "Today, rather than reflecting on the past, we're embracing our future—"

Blah, blah, blah.

I checked out. Glancing to my tab, I scrolled through the electronic textbook. What was Eliza talking about? I knew history. Pilgrims to the new land: Little men in funny clothes didn't like the king's rules and wanted to go to their own kind of church. Launch a boat, sail the big ol' blue, and start a whole new life. Check. Revolutionary War: Rich white guys wearing ridiculous wigs decided they didn't want to answer to King George, so they dumped some tea into a harbor, which inexplicably made the king mad. Royal Navy versus ragtag Patriots, and somehow the little guys came out on top. Hello, America. Check. Civil War: Abe said slavery was bad. The Southern states said he couldn't tell them what to do. Boom, you had a war. The North won. Bye-bye slavery. Check, again. The Bloody Faith Conflict: Some extremists from the East attacked three major US cities and the midwestern breadbasket. America took the fight to them. Global response wasn't favorable to the deportation and blank-slate annihilation policies, and boom, we had severe economic collapse. Enter the Progressive Party. Final check. Let's move on.

See, I knew my history. Eliza didn't know what she was talking about.

What was she saying about end times? Clearly she didn't

think this was it. Then why was she all psycho about everything? And how did she know it wasn't the end? Didn't Jesus say that no man knew the dates and times?

Eliza could frustrate me like no one else. Which meant, contrary to popular belief, she wasn't dull. That made me smile.

Our friendship was an interesting match. I was a pop-bottle rocket, easily lit, short fused, and more noise than show. Eliza was a sunrise. Quiet, slow, reliable. And yet every day a wonder. Most people thought our *best friends* status was covertly more than best friends, and I wouldn't have minded if that were true—but Eliza didn't live by social standards. *Dating is a path to marriage*, she said, *not a recreational sport.* See, quirky, right? But tolerable. No, adorable. And I had to admit, she lived by her words, which was rare and demanded some respect.

Sadly, all this made her a big fat bull's-eye for guys like Hulk. Locker-room talk was hardly G-rated, and when it had turned to Eliza Knight at the beginning of football season, the bets started rolling. I came home with my second broken nose in September, dealt by the hand of a senior who'd wagered his ability to *charm the unsoiled.* My cool evaporated like a mist on hot asphalt. I had come out on the bottom, but nobody brought her up again. Close enough to a win.

Eliza didn't know about any of that.

"Dismissed."

Mr. Nigel's release drifted through my wandering thoughts, and I flipped my tab shut. First hour gone. On to conquer English.

I didn't see Eliza the rest of the day. The smart kids got to stay in the nice end of the school, and our lunches weren't during the same hour. I figured she'd settle by tomorrow morning though—barring any bus incidents.

I missed riding the bus with her after school, which sadly we still did because public transport permits weren't cheap, especially if you were under twenty-one, but I had football practice. An athletic scholarship was my only other hope for higher education. That was a slender thread too, but I had the Luther name going for me. That was something, at least. Anyway, the season would be done in three more weeks, and then I'd be back to our normal routine. Twenty-minute bus ride, walk Eliza to her door, and then hope my dad wasn't working on his sermon at home. Crikey. Once a week was enough.

I threw on my practice uniform and jogged to the football field in the midst of a steady stream of my teammates. Reaching the sideline, I put out a hand to snatch my yellow special-team's jersey. I had the profound honor of playing back-up punter. Amazing, huh? I was really going to have to work that name angle, because an athletic slot at the university level based on my talent, not to mention playing time, would require the death of most males between the ages of sixteen and eighteen sometime in the next four years.

I needed to study harder.

"Luther, wear a white." Coach hardly looked at me as he barked from the sideline.

"A white?" I stammered. Where exactly was I supposed to set up on the offensive line?

Coach shot a look at me like...like I was bear bait. "Left tackle."

Crikey. There was a reason I didn't play O-line—something about the string-bean problem. And left tackle? I couldn't play blind side. What was the man thinking?

Shaking, but hoping it looked more like adrenaline rather than absolute terror, I lined up directly across from Hulk.

"You're gonna die, PK."

Probably. Wish I'd known about this before I'd lipped off earlier.

Somewhere in the distance, I heard the count, and then the call, and then I felt Hulk's massive body slam me onto the turf, which at that particular moment felt more like cement. My helmet flew loose, but as I reached for it, a muscled arm sent my chin backward. I felt the collision of my head and the ground, and everything went black.

A high-pitched squeal rang in my ears when I tried to focus my eyes. The afternoon sunlight shot screaming pain to the center of my brain as I tried to collect reality. I couldn't have been out that long, because Hulk still hovered over me.

"There's a Party shirt in your locker, PK." He held my shoulder down and hunkered lower. "I'd wear it tomorrow or skip practice. I told you—it's a new age."

—————

I went to check on Eliza after I'd showered, but not to tell her about the practice incident. I wanted to tell her because the whole deal was really weird, and I usually told her everything, but this was just too creepy. Coaches got pretty uptight about cheap shots—fouls cost yards and lose games—but Coach didn't say a thing. Didn't even ask if I was all right, which was also strange. Head injuries got treated like heart attacks. Not a word about it though.

Maybe Eliza had been onto something. I started suspecting Coach's political allegiances lay with Kasen Asend. And I was Braxton Luther, Patrick Luther's son. My father was a pretty well-known preacher around here. Even had a syndicated broadcast of his sermons, though his audience had steadily dwindled over my lifetime. Perhaps there was more trouble mixed up with this election than I'd thought. But telling Eliza what happened would have made her lose more sleep, and that didn't seem right, so I determined to swallow it and move on.

Eliza answered her front door after I'd knocked the second time. "Hey, what's going on?"

I shrugged, hoping my ringing head and the pain zipping up and down my neck didn't show in my expression. "You were pretty upset today. I wanted to make sure you're okay."

"Really?" Her eyes looked watery. Weird. Eliza didn't cry. I'd seen her wreck her bike, slamming her chin onto the handlebars. She didn't cry. She wasn't the weepy type.

"Really," I said. Was that a lie? Nah—I did want to know that she was okay. "You're not though. Want to talk?"

She gawked at me. I think if I'd kissed her, she wouldn't have been more dumbfounded.

"Come on." I turned and stepped down her front porch. On the sidewalk, I waited for her to snap her mouth closed and follow me.

We circled her big backyard, continuing past the white picket fence toward the creek that slithered behind our neighborhood. The whole area had been a dairy farm once, belonging to Eliza's grandparents. I didn't know why they sold it, but this part had been developed into a subdivision. The creek and about fifty yards of this side of its bank had been left as open space. The other side sprawled into a forest, untouched by the modern world. I wasn't sure who owned it— I'd suspected Eliza's family, but she'd never said so, and I thought it'd be rude to ask. See, sometimes I could think beyond myself. Rarely.

We neared the bank, and I plopped under an oak. The spot was sacred—we'd met there. After my family had moved to Glennbrooke eight years ago, I'd followed the creek to this tree and then climbed it. Eliza was sitting in the crook of a branch, hidden from view until I'd scaled to her position. We'd spent the rest of that summer there. Playing. Pretending to fish in the narrow stream. Climbing trees. And planting a forever friendship.

Maybe that was strange—an eight-year-old boy finding his best friend in a girl hiding in a tree and holding on to her for the next eight years—but I'd been the new kid. More significantly, the new kid who happened to be the son of the famous Patrick Luther, football star, outspoken Christian athlete-turned-pastor. The man people loved—and hated. My father had just taken the pulpit in a large church in his former hometown. He'd been given a hero's homecoming and then slid back into what I assumed had been his old fame. I needed something to call my own, a place to belong. Eliza was it. Something like that carved loyalty deep, even in a sixteen-year-old guy.

I slouched against the rough bark of the tree, and Eliza sat across from me. She squinted, tilting her head to one side. "What's wrong with your eyes?"

"What?"

"They're not right." She leaned in closer. "One is dilated more than the other. Did you hit your head?"

"Yeah, but I'm fine."

"No you're not."

"Eliza, stop." I took her shoulders and pushed her back so she couldn't examine my apparently concussed head. "How did you know about the rally Friday?"

"You wouldn't believe all the things you can hear when you're *not* talking." She eyed me, and then her head bobbed forward with a small laugh. She settled a crooked smile on me —her teasing expression—and then turned serious again. "There are whispers everywhere, even in church. This is a defining election. People are still mad about the market collapse after the war. Mad because the American involvement in the war was religious. Mad at the government because the choices made during and after that time made the dollar worthless on a global market. I mean, look at everything that was lost. Free education—at least the valued kind. The chance for everyone to chase their dreams. Big, nice houses. College open to everyone, and often funded by government subsidies. Now what do you see when we ride the bus to school? We have to test into our places in school, and our parents have to pay for our spots. The nice houses in town are either owned by the elite or are completely boarded up and abandoned. My dad—he sees some pretty crazy stuff in healthcare. He even has to treat things like scurvy. Scurvy! Because the poor people can't afford fruits and vegetables in a limited market and a land largely damaged by war. We're lucky, Braxton. We live like we haven't been touched by the collapse. But other people? They believe in the equalizing promises of the Progressive Party because they're desperate for hope."

Quite a speech by the quiet and thoughtful Eliza Knight. By the time she finished, the frenzy of panic edged her voice again.

I jammed my hand into my coarse hair—the one Luther trait I managed to inherit. "I still don't understand you. What are you afraid of?"

"Someone's gotta take the blame for the fallout of the last twenty-five years, Braxton."

"Who?"

"Take a guess."

"Christians? Why?"

"Not just Christians. Religion." Eliza sighed. "Because of the Conflict. People think it wouldn't have happened if religion hadn't been a part of our culture. The Progressives hate that we still cling to God. They're afraid of it."

I shook my head. "There's got to be a better reason than that."

"The Party has a whole list of reasons—starting at the top with *He's imaginary and not the boss of me*—but it all boils down to a hatred for God. Hatred of people who would still believe in a god after everything that happened."

Eliza and theological debates. I huffed. "So what about this rally?"

"I already told you what I know." She held a long look on me and then scowled. "You told me not to worry about it. Why are you suddenly so interested?"

I didn't think very far in advance. If I had, I would have known she'd expect an explanation, which meant telling her about practice. I plucked at the cool grass, now mostly brown by the hand of several killing frosts, fumbling around in my head for something that would satisfy Eliza.

"Someone left a Party shirt in my locker." The muted truth. It would do. "I've got the idea I'm expected to wear it."

Rather than surprise, Eliza's eyebrow quirked in challenge. "Are you going to?"

That was indeed the question.

CHAPTER THREE

AN INJURY ENDED THE FOOTBALL SEASON FOR ME. GUESS Hulk had been serious. I didn't explain it all to Eliza, because it would terrify her. Or to my parents—they wouldn't notice anyway. My father always had his face stuck in a book or was engrossed in his sermons, if he wasn't off saving the world one sinner at a time, and Mom...well, she hadn't been the same since we'd moved.

It took months for my most-likely-cracked ribs to heal, and I was pretty sure my back would never be right again. I wondered why I had even played in the first place. Another letdown to contrast against the great Luther success. And yet, I kept trying. Inexplicable.

Kasen Asend was sworn into office in January. The festivities of Inauguration Day, a holiday previously unnoticed by the average teenaged Joe, exceeded those of the Fourth of July. School was canceled. Fireworks flew. And the Party celebrated.

After that things started to settle, and I shifted back into my original claim. Everything would blow over—Kasen made his figurehead move, and now real life would slide back into normal. And it did.

Spring sprung, flowers bloomed, and our six-week summer break rolled around. I relaxed, and Eliza did too. She stopped wearing her *we're doomed* expression, stopped insisting we stay at all the prayer meetings my father called, and began to look forward to a normal future.

Until the letter came.

Eliza had to retest her Career Track. The form claimed all Career Track students had to be reevaluated. The slots had been cut, and to be fair, all students had to take the test again before the positions would be filled. She would have to travel to the state center—at the expense of her parents. And she'd be alone. LiteRail travel wasn't cheap. Her parents couldn't afford to go with her.

I ignored the pinch of concern in my stomach the day she left. Eliza was the smartest person I knew. She'd be fine.

She came back the day after her test, which was a week before our break was to end. I met her at our oak tree that afternoon. "Well?"

"It was the same test." She shrugged, but she wasn't confident. "Mostly."

"Perfect. You're in."

She didn't bloom in my confidence, but we moved on. Summer shouldn't be wasted on worry. Sixteen and ambitious, we were way too young to be treading in the murky depths of concern. We walked down to the church and played foosball the rest of the afternoon, which was effective—for me. I forgot about her test.

The Friday before our junior year began, I found Eliza sitting by the creek, her knees pulled up, arms wrapped around them and head tucked down. If I didn't know her better, I'd have thought she was crying.

She was. She lifted her head as I approached. Tiny drops of water dotted her sun-kissed cheeks. I'd never seen that before.

"What happened?" I dropped across from her in the grass.

"I didn't make it."

Make what? My blank stare must have communicated my dim wit.

"I didn't pass into the Career Track."

"What?" Impossible. Completely impossible. She'd tested into the ninety-ninth percentile the last time. No way she didn't pass.

Eliza stiffened, swiped at her cheeks, and that was the last of her tears. Tears. From Eliza? She was serious.

"What happened?"

"I got a form letter simply stating that I didn't qualify." Her jaw moved like she was setting a clamp on her emotion.

"But you said it was the same test."

"It was, mostly."

Yeah, that was exactly what she'd said. I looked at her with my *keep talking* expression.

Her bottom lip quivered. "The top form was different."

"The top form?" I tried to remember a top form on the test I'd taken two years before.

"Yeah, you know the profile form that they use for statistics?" She unlocked her knees and leaned back on her hands.

I scowled, shaking my head.

"Where it asks your age, and parents' income range, and you have to check a box to define your race—Caucasian, Hispanic, African American. Remember?"

"Oh yeah, I'm with you." Except I had no idea why that mattered for her test score.

"There's a new category now."

"Of race?"

"No, of political alignment. Two boxes to choose from: Progressive Reform Party or Traditionalist."

I bet she didn't mark the Progressive box.

"You have to ask to retake the test." It was the only way. Eliza had a future—a good one. And our country needed her brains and her compassion in the medical field. She couldn't give up.

"You're not listening, Braxton. I could have gotten every question on that test right. It wouldn't matter—"

"I *am* listening." I leaned in closer, my voice hot. "Change your answer on one question, and you're in."

Her eyes flashed, and her expression widened like I'd just asked her to strip naked in front of me or something equally immoral. Somehow I felt dirty. I pulled in a lungful of air, unsure as to why I was upset with her. "Play the game, Liza. It's just a piece of paper."

She drew back and then scowled. "So is the Declaration of Independence."

"It's not like that." I huffed. "Look, God knows your heart. Stay faithful on the inside. He wants you to be successful— why else would He have made you so smart? Check the box. Move on with your life."

Her eyes locked on me with resolve so strong that I felt my own weakness tremble.

"No." She held me pinned under her disapproval for one more breath and then stood to walk away.

Her answer rung in my ears for the rest of the day, and on Monday, it returned like a haunting whisper.

I changed in the locker room after school, just like a normal day. Training camp for football started that afternoon, and I geared up for another four months of punting. I might actually make the first squad this year, because the guy I had played behind graduated.

"Luther, in my office," Coach bellowed into the cavernous locker room. I'd never been summoned before. I hoped he'd caught wind that I'd improved my longest kick by fifteen yards over the break. First string for sure.

I barely cast my shadow through the door before he spoke.

"You're out, boy." He didn't even glance at me.

Excuse me—did I just get cut? "What?"

"Don't want to waste your time." He continued shuffling his lineup charts and plays on his clipboard. "You're done. Turn in your practice uniform by the end of the week."

The room went out of focus. "Wh-why?"

He stopped his fidgeting and looked at me over the rim of his glasses. He didn't breathe another word—and he didn't need to. I knew why.

Blood rushed through my head, and heat sizzled in my veins. "This is political, isn't it?"

"Not another word, PK."

PK? A high school football coach called me PK—as in preacher's kid—after he'd cut me from the team? This had to be so illegal.

"Do you think I'll stand by quietly while you single me out for going to church?" There went my mouth again.

He dropped his clipboard onto his desk and squared his large body to mine. Bushy eyebrows dropped low over his eyes, which flashed with some kind of heat. "I expect you'll fall in line, boy. You and your father both. It's a new age, and you need to come to terms with that." He held his glare for one more silent, blistering moment. "Now get out of here. Get your head on straight."

Cut from the team—and not for my mediocrity. For my church affiliation. And Eliza, barred from the coveted Career Track. None of this could be legal. Setting aside the whole dollar-sign issue, we had to find a way to file a court case.

I had to talk to my father about it. That was maybe the worst part of the whole deal. Approaching him was something like requesting an appointment with the president, and I hated that. A son was supposed to come to his dad for anything, right? Shouldn't have to be punched into his schedule in order to have a chat. But this...this was a big deal. Important enough to take the gut shot.

Except it didn't happen. When I got home that night, the news was on, and my parents were glued to it. Didn't even notice I walked in two hours earlier than usual.

"Hey, son." Mother spoke on autopilot. "How was your day?"

Same question, in the same tone, with the same distracted look I got every day.

I dropped my pack on the kitchen table. "Uh, different." Turning back, I waited for either of them to respond.

Their attention stayed riveted on some raging fire pictured on the screen. I glanced to it. Black smoke billowed against a blue sky someplace where trees didn't grow very thick and the ground remained pretty level. A serious-sounding woman relayed the details while the picture continued to show different angles of the huge blaze. "The initial explosion set off a chain reaction, and the resulting wildfire continues to rage. All remaining residents have been evacuated, and because of the possible radioactive leak, officials are evacuating a massive radius. Now labeled the Vacant Plains after the ravages of the

Bloody Faith Conflict, the heart of the country looks to be completely uninhabitable..."

Nothing was ever good in the news.

I cleared my throat. "Uh, Dad...can I talk to you?"

"Not now."

Of course not. I hadn't called first. Who was I to compete with some dumb explosion that happened hundreds of miles away?

Skip it. They didn't need to know.

The rest of the week slugged by—the only good part being that Eliza and I had some of the same classes now that she'd been demoted to the dummy ranks. Even at that, scowls directed at us, and at a few other known *churchies*, as well as a few under-the-breath warnings about "falling in line," made school...uncomfortable.

By Sunday, confusion had blown into full-scale fear. Service attendance had slimmed down to less than half, making our large trendy sanctuary feel like a modern stage hosting a bad band. Father called a prayer meeting immediately after service.

"Let's go," I whispered to Eliza, nudging her shoulder.

"No."

She was getting pretty consistent with that monosyllable stake in the ground.

I tugged on her elbow. "We need to talk. I need some answers."

She pulled free from my fingers. "We need to pray. We can talk later."

My mouth sagged, and all I could do was look at her.

So, we prayed. Only thirty people stayed. My father led, and when he finished, most of those scurried out like they hoped they wouldn't get caught.

"What will we do?" An elderly voice asked from the front. Mr. Harper. Pretty sure he'd been a part of this congregation since the Tower of Babel.

My father didn't falter. "We'll continue."

Jedidiah Stevens stood, folding his arms over his chest. "What about the pew tax?"

Pew tax?

"We're not enforcing it." Father held a steady challenge on the burly man.

Jed frowned, taking a wide stance. "How do you reckon the church will keep afloat if we're paying an attendance fee every Sunday?"

Not many challenged Father. Especially around here. His build and intellect usually had a subduing effect on people, and let's not forget his fame. He'd played college football once upon a time. A local talent who became one of the standouts in the national elite conference. Rumors had him in the pro draft, even going first round. He opted to go to seminary instead. After that, he'd taken a pulpit in the Pacific Northwest, grew a megachurch, and then left Jamis to carry on his successful pastorate so he could return to his midwestern hometown. Except, from what I could figure from the bits of conversation I managed to pick up between my parents, now that church was also a minichurch, but that wasn't Jamis's fault. Of course. All the while, my father, the superhero-football-player preacher, never lost his imposing presence—defying the stereotyped minuscule preacher-man image.

Father proved why most skulked away from him in a disagreement. Broad shoulders squared on Jed, he seemed to ripple with strength. "I don't know. But I'll not allow the Party to hold a ransom on the gospel. I'm not charging people to hear the Word of God."

"Then you have sentenced this congregation." Jed slid into his chair as he spoke.

Sentenced it to what? I leaned into Eliza. "What's he talking about?"

She looked at me sideways, her eyebrow hiked into her forehead. "You need to pay attention, Braxton."

"I *am* paying attention."

Her hand wrapped around mine, and she stood. "Come on." She dropped it as soon as we were moving, and we shuffled off to the youth room. Even in the deserted space, with the door closed, she whispered. "Braxton, you've got to start listening to what is going on."

"I heard. Pew tax. What is that?"

"This is what I'm talking about. How do you *not* know?" She shook her head like I was unbelievably ignorant. "Earlier this week President Asend appointed a new justice for the Supreme Court. His second appointment in eight months. Second, Braxton. Do you understand how important that is?"

I flinched—because I didn't really get it, and I hated feeling dumb. "No."

"It means that the Party has control of the Supreme Court. They already had control of the Legislature." Eliza stopped, as though she were gauging how much my tiny brain was absorbing.

Not much.

"Do you understand how our government works?"

Insulted as I was—because I knew I was supposed to understand—I stood there muted.

"Three branches, Braxton. That's what makes it work—the checks and balances of the three branches is supposed to ensure that the government stays balanced, that no one ever gains absolute power."

A glimmer of comprehension shafted in my dim mind. "But the Party has?"

"They've got the whole tree by the trunk."

That wasn't possible. Not in this country. The land of the free and the home of the brave—our people wouldn't stand to be ruled by a tyrant. Would they?

Anyway, Eliza still hadn't answered my real question. "What does that have to do with a pew tax?"

"It was signed into law this week." Eliza's shoulders sagged, and she leaned her back against the wall. Sliding to the floor, she took the form of a bunny, cornered and afraid. "After Asend's justice appointment was approved by the legislature. The new tax was part of the Religious Emancipation Act."

So, I wasn't smart, but I knew the word *emancipation*. Eliza must have misunderstood. "That means freedom. Freedom of religion, which has always been a part of American government."

"One little word can change the whole meaning." She looked up at me, misery radiating from her face. "Freedom *from* religion. That's how it reads now."

I stared at her and then laughed. "That's impossible."

She sat a little straighter. "What's impossible is how much you *don't* pay attention." She scowled, lifting her chin with a challenge she only ever used with me. "Why have you been getting home so early this week, Braxton? What happened to practice?"

How the heck did she know that? I'd skipped riding the bus just so I wouldn't have to explain anything to anyone.

"You think I don't see you walking back by the creek. Hiding." Standing up, the frightened rabbit transformed into a fearless bulldog. "Tell me. What happened?"

I swallowed. I hated making her mad—it was so contrary to

her nature. But at the same time, she could make me furious. So perfect. Smart. Good. Always made the right choices. Always said the right thing. Her life highlighted all my inadequacies, like a blotch of ketchup on a white T-shirt.

Every muscle in my body went rigid. "I was cut. All right?"

She didn't flinch. "Why?"

"Because I'm not my dad." My voice filled the room.

"You know that's not why." She lifted her chin and took a step toward me. "You're better than you were last year. You *know* why. Say it."

I couldn't, which seemed contrary to my nature. Here I had an opportunity—a legitimate door—to blame my failure on someone else, and I couldn't do it. Because admitting what Eliza was implying spun a thick web of terror inside me. It couldn't be right. She had to be dead wrong.

Eliza waited, her breath even, with a faint glow from our confrontation on her cheeks. "Why did I get cut from the Career Track, Braxton? Why does the church have to report attendance and pay for the occupied spaces? Why were you cut from the football team?"

My tongue glued to the roof of my mouth. I could do the math. But saying it out loud felt like...like treason.

"You can't ride the fence forever." Her eyes inexplicably softened, and her hand rested on my arm. "It's only going to get worse."

CHAPTER FOUR

By November, I was beginning to think Eliza had been endowed with the gift of prophecy. Worse kept coming.

Snow fluttered in the icy air the day our power cut out. The entire house went black. By nightfall we'd all doubled our layers of clothing. The low was expected to dip below zero, and the wind had already picked up. Our generator ran on fossil fuel, which we hadn't been able to buy for two months, and we didn't have a wood-burning stove.

Bundling in our winter's warmest, my mother, father, and I trudged down to the Knights'. Porch lights gleamed from houses along the way, their glow sparking anger in my gut. Father had refused to enforce the pew tax—if he'd charged for an audience, he wouldn't have one. So he must have paid the government from his salary. Though the congregation dwindled, it still had to have been costly. And now our power had been unplugged.

Eliza's house was warm—but the heat smelled of hickory and was centralized around their fireplace, the focal point of their living room. Jayla Knight welcomed us all into her home with the kind of warmth that characterized Eliza. Clearly Ms. Knight had passed on so much more than her Hispanic heritage—dark hair, rich brown eyes, and creamy tanned skin—to her oldest daughter.

Hannah sat on the opposite end of the room from Eliza, huddled in a thick blanket and clearly working at *not* looking at me. Good kid, usually—although a tad annoying, because she was often a tagalong. She had a crush on me, which she tried her hardest to hide. Had to admit, the girl's admiration kind of tripped a billow of satisfaction through me. Who didn't like being crushed on? Sad, though, it seemed to cause a crack between the two sisters.

"Have you heard from Jamis and Annyon?" Jayla asked my mother in a hushed tone.

Mother's eyes glazed, and she blinked. "Jamis wrote several weeks ago. His congregation is flagging. We can't contact either of them anymore though. It's too expensive." She looked down and tried to muffle a sniff. "Annyon..."

I looked away. Mother's AWOL son—her pride and joy—bringing her to tears. Not something I wanted to witness. I pushed my gloved hands toward the fire's glow, and Eliza came to my side.

"Your lights are still on." I spoke low so our conversation stayed between us. "Why are you heating the house with wood?"

"We have been for a month." She hugged herself, and I saw the cuff of a long-sleeved shirt under her sweater. "Daddy shut off the furnace. Said it's more important to be able to cook than to have cozy bedrooms. And we only use this front room light and the kitchen light for a couple of hours a day. He's hoping the money will stretch until spring."

Their money needed stretching? "Why?"

Eliza shivered. "The taxes hit hard."

I thought my father wasn't enforcing the pew tax.

Coming from the kitchen, just off the living area, Eliza's mom handed me a bowl. Steam drifted from the hot broth and root veggies to my nose. I missed red meat, but my gurgling stomach demanded to be filled. Eliza folded her legs under her, sitting on the floor near the warmth of the fire with her own bowl of soup. I took the space beside her, my mind still searching for answers.

Heat from the warm bowl seeped into my fingers, and I delayed eating, hoping my hands would thaw. "What happens in the spring?"

"What do you mean?"

"You said your father hoped the money would stretch until spring," I said. Hunger overrode my still-cold fingers, and I took a spoonful of soup to my mouth. Bland broth disappointed my tongue—vegetable, without much salt.

"I don't know." Eliza sipped her soup from the bowl. "Probably just something to look forward to. I don't think anything will change much politically—at least not for the better. We'll be able to grow things though." She took another drink from her bowl and then stared into the fire.

I imagined the dormant garden plots carved into the yards over in the poverty area of town. The image didn't fit in the Knights' nicely landscaped and well-kept yard.

"Have you heard about the rallies?" Eliza asked, bringing my mind back to the broth and fireplace.

I'd have to have my head in the creek *not* to hear about the rallies. They happened as often as the football games—and usually right after. I didn't go to either. Life had become a monotonous pattern of school and then home, with church thrown in on Sundays. All the other extra stuff, Bible studies and board meetings and prayer gatherings, had come to a dead stop. No one, except Eliza's father and Mr. Harper, ever came anymore. Several months before, Jedidiah Stevens had, with a mask of condescending authority, told everyone that continuing such *engagements* was no longer wise.

I wondered if Jedidiah went to the rallies.

"There are more tattoos." Eliza's eyes remained fixed on the blaze in the fireplace. "Everywhere. I've even seen them in church. They're calling it a *Citizen's Seal*." She shifted, looking to me.

Her gaze implored me about things I couldn't answer. Would I get one? I had a reasonable suspicion it would make life easier. At least at school. It wouldn't turn the heat back on in my house though. Or give my parents any means of financial relief.

No. No, I wouldn't do it. Especially if it made Eliza look at me like that—like I'd taken a piece of her friendship, the piece that trusted me, that admired me, and thrown it into the sewer.

"I don't even go to the rallies, Liza." I ducked away from her probing look. "Don't think that about me."

She seemed to exhale. Was my character that questionable? I searched her profile, wanting to probe her, but also afraid of what she might say.

"There's a new act on the table in Washington." My attention diverted to Eliza's father, who sat on the couch across the room, his shoulders hunched over as though he carried the earth upon his back.

"The Citizen Recharacterization Act." My father nodded, his solemn voice matching his downcast face. "The government will provide all promised benefits to any legitimized citizen of the US, without expense." He shook his head. "Someone's got to pay for it."

"We already *are* paying for it." Mother's low voice surged with resentment. "The new tax brackets will break us before anyone will see any benefits."

"Benefits won't go to everyone if that act is passed." Jayla Knight spoke softly from a chair near my place on the floor. She sounded defeated, like there really wasn't an *if* in that scenario. "It'll redefine citizenship. Not everyone will qualify."

"How will citizenship be defined?" Words tumbled out of my mouth before I realized it.

All eyes settled on me. Was it another stupid question?

Father shuddered. It was subtle, but I saw it. My stomach knotted, hard and queasy. I'd never, in all my seventeen years, seen him actually quiver with fear.

"Whoever is in compliance with the Party will be granted citizenship." He spoke to the floor. This man hunched over, almost whispering, was my father? The man who had played the offensive line in college? Whose booming voice required no microphone from the pulpit? They turned off our power, and he bowed to the disgrace—without a fight. Without a plan.

The stone in my gut hardened. I wouldn't bow, not like that. They could define citizenship however they wanted. I wouldn't let them rip away my life. Politics was a game of hide and seek. If they wanted to hide the American Dream, I'd find the stores of prosperity. Only fools clung to their ideology, exchanging success for misery.

I caught Eliza looking at me, the same penetrating questions from our earlier conversation lurking in her eyes. *The Citizen's Seal.* Suddenly, I understood. And I couldn't answer her unvoiced question anymore.

———

We stayed at the Knights' house—which was a little awkward when it was your best-female-friend's house and you were the pastor's son. None of us advertised the situation, but word got out. It just did.

"Getting cozy with the church girl, eh PK?"

I didn't know how Hulk had managed to permanently tag us with those names even though he'd graduated the spring before, but I'd heard that line at least two thousand times by the time Friday rolled around. I should have done more to guard Eliza, but I only ducked my head and walked the other way. How she handled it, I don't know. We never talked about it.

Tension pulled on all of us. Sleeping on the floor, eating in a crowded room because every other room in the house was cold, and dealing with the harassment—all of it knuckled us down tight. I needed a break. From my mother's worried eyes. My father's heavy spirit. And Eliza's consuming, silent pleas.

Be strong. Don't bend. I could pretty much hear her thoughts every evening as we drank our tasteless broth.

You can't ride the fence. I could see the admonition in her eyes every time she turned them to me.

We can't live like this, I would argue back in my head. I was pretty sure she could read me too.

I stayed at school after classes let out on Friday. The last home game started at six. It was my first and only game of the season. I didn't watch much of it. Just sat at the top of the stands and listened, thinking about how Eliza had said that you could learn a lot when you were quiet. She was right.

"Ten more tonight," said some kid in the bleachers below me. "They've signed the oath, and the inker is coming."

The entire football team had been branded. I could see their marks from my spot in the stands. Every neck had been inked with the circle containing the fist and sledgehammer. Words arched over the top of the Party's symbol. I couldn't read them from that distance, but I was pretty sure they said *By our hands*. I rubbed my neck, wondering if the ink needle hurt.

"The Stevens kid is coming," a girl added. She was a junior. I think her name was Ashley. She'd been to church a handful of times, but she'd never come to youth group. "His dad is sending some kindling. He was inked last month."

I knew it. Jedidiah had been bad news even when things had been good.

I pulled my coat closer and tried to focus on the game.

"Hey, PK." The kid below me turned around. I recognized him from first-hour history. "Are you staying tonight?"

My blood froze. The whole row of students turned to look at me. Most were from the Career Track. I didn't really know them. A few had gone to our church, the Christmas, Easter, and funeral types. Three I recognized from my classes. But the other faces in the crowd—didn't know them. So many in our school were new, recently allowed to enroll under the Party's Citizen Benefits Implementation. I suspected that had something to do with the Recharacterization Act my parents were stewing about. Especially since every new student looked on the low end of poor and bore the inked seal of the Party.

Ashley grazed a condescending looked me over. "You're from that noncompliant church, aren't you?"

Noncompliant?

"Yeah." History-class boy nodded to her. "That's PK—as in pastor's kid. Pastor Luther."

"Your church is in rebellion." Ashley cocked an eyebrow. "Maybe you'd better stay. It would improve your...civic standing."

I had a civic standing? I thought it was a social standing, and it hadn't been much to begin with.

My mouth went dry, while my heart throbbed. Eliza. I could see her in my mind. The disappointment in her eyes. The disapproval in her set jaw.

But she didn't know what went on at a rally. Neither of us did. How could we be so sure it was bad if we'd never been before?

"You could even get sealed." Ashley tipped a challenging grin. "The inker is coming, and there are always Party officials around—who could take your oath. Rumor has it that Stateswoman Charlotte Sanger will be here tonight. It'd be a good night to make a new statement." She winked and added a little sultry to her smile.

Not a chance. Mostly because Eliza would hate me. And my father—he'd go off. Though seventeen, I was still scared of my dad when he got mad. He was no flimsy fool, and I was no match for his brains or brawn.

Still, I didn't have to get sealed. I could just hang around and see what all the hoopla was about. That couldn't hurt—and like Ashley said, it might actually help. All of us.

Somewhere in my silence, the group below me lost interest. I landed back on the fence without their beckoning, without their challenging stares. By the end of the game, I'd talked myself out of it. Eliza would worry, and explaining where I was to my father didn't sound like a fun Friday night activity.

History-class boy stood at the last whistle and turned my direction. "Come on, PK. Stay a spell. Who knows—it might even help your family's electrical issues." His wiry smile hinted conspiracy.

How could my going to some stupid bonfire help turn our

lights back on? I was pretty sure that was a money issue, not a civic issue. The question rolled around in my head while the group gawked in my direction.

"Let's go." Ashley tipped her head toward the field. "We'll even call you by your real name, Braxton." She smiled, her wink both scintillating and sinister.

I wasn't sure if it was their persistence or my curiosity that got me, but before I really understood my decision, I stood on the field in the midst of a growing crowd. The football players, both teams, reemerged from the locker rooms without their gear. Adults rivaled the students in population. And very few necks lacked the Citizen's Seal. I huddled into my coat, pretending I was cold so that I wouldn't feel like such a coward.

Andre Stevens crossed my path of vision, his backpack bulging at the zipper and looking painfully heavy. "Here's enough to get us started." His cheery call drifted over the crowd as he unzipped the pack. Books dropped to the turf. Leather bound, hard backed, paperback. They landed helter skelter, pages bent and spines pressed the wrong way. Andre kicked them, and other kids picked several volumes up and threw them into a ring of dirt and ash just beyond the north end zone.

A title glittered in the fluorescent lamplight, demanding my attention and twisting my stomach.

The Holy Bible.

Andre had brought the Bible to throw into the bonfire. God's Word. They were burning God's Word.

Other students had arrived, laden with heavy packs. All of them stuffed with books. The Torah. The Book of Mormon. The Quran. And more Bibles, along with well-known literary contributors to the world's major religions. Several I didn't recognize, but there were authors I knew from my father's study. Luther, Calvin, Spurgeon, Piper, MacArthur, Bonhoeffer, to name a few.

The stack grew, and then a torch arrived. A strong musty smell mingled with the pungent odor of fire, and a bluish haze began to fill the field. Flames licked the books like an evil tongue while a roar lifted from the crowd.

"By our hands. By our hands. By our hands."

Eliza had been right. It was a statement of defiance. Fists shook to the heavens, faces upturned toward the sky. Mocking. Shouting. Rebelling.

My gut burned as if the fire had leapt from the pages of the Bible and scalded my soul. Tightness in my chest made it hard to breathe, and I couldn't think past the need to flee. Get away. Far, far away.

I wanted nothing to do with the Party. Ever.

CHAPTER FIVE

Eliza asked me where I'd been.

"In the woods." Sort of true. I walked home through them, hoping I hadn't been noticed leaving the rally, that I wouldn't be seen going home.

She held me with a look that said *I know when you're lying*. I swear, sometimes she could see into my soul.

"Did we win?" She skipped the whole *you're not being honest* part, which was one of the reasons I liked her.

My father would fish around with a three-pronged hook, snagging onto every lie I'd ever told in my life, and then say, "Now tell me the truth." That was never effective, because by the time he got there, I was so dang mad that he could threaten to remove my tongue and I still wouldn't tell him. Because I was stubborn, and I didn't like to be pushed around.

"Yeah. They won." I took the bowl she passed to me and stared at the translucent brown liquid.

Eliza sat beside me, both of us on the floor close to the fire. The room was empty except the two of us—Hannah and both sets of parents were sleeping, I guessed, because it was pretty late. Though alone with Eliza, I felt the crowd pressing in close, their jeers throbbing toward heaven. Piercing my soul. A tremble raced over me.

"What's the rally like?" Eliza whispered, as though speaking of it might be costly. Or maybe she was afraid someone in the house might still be awake.

I sat unmoving, almost in a trance. "Awful."

Her eyes settled on me—I could feel her examining my face. "You smell funny."

"Marijuana." I turned to her, still feeling shaken and... debased. "I'm pretty sure it's marijuana."

"Did you—"

"No." I hated that she even asked. "It was everywhere though."

"Wow. That sounds crazy." She waited.

I did nothing.

"Braxton, you're being weird. Are you sure you didn't—"

"I'm not high," I snapped. I put the bowl of soup, which I hadn't touched, on the floor and crammed my hand through my hair. "They were burning books." I glared at her, still seeing the fire consuming the pages. "Bibles—and other holy books. They were burning them."

Her eyes widened. "Like Nazis?"

Leave it to Eliza to refer to something that happened more than a hundred years ago. "I guess."

She chomped on her bottom lip, taking the situation in. Or maybe trying not say *I told you so*.

"What else?"

That wasn't enough? "They were saying ten more were getting sealed tonight—that the inker was coming, and they actually did it there, during the rally."

"Do they always do that?"

I shrugged. Didn't think about it. Didn't know if it mattered. All I knew was that I didn't want to be there, or anywhere near there. "We should leave."

"Leave?" Eliza scrunched her face like I'd lost my mind. "It's past midnight. We can't leave."

"Not now." I spun my backside on the floor to face her. "That's not what I mean. There's some kind of crazy frenzy happening here. We should move, go away. I'm not sure we're safe here."

Her eyebrows lifted, and she shook her head. "Braxton, you're still not getting this." She leaned closer. "It's not just here. It's everywhere. The Party has swept the nation—we won't be able to get away from this."

"How do you know?" I tilted toward her too, our faces close enough to feel the heat of the other's breath. "We haven't been anywhere else. Maybe it's just this town. Maybe there's somewhere with some sanity still left on the streets. You can't know."

She gripped my elbow. "I've been somewhere." The intensity in her voice matched the firm hold she had on my arm. "Remember? I took the LiteRail. I went to the state center. Tattoos, posters, chants on the streets—it was everywhere. And remember what your mom said about Jamis's church? It's failing, just like ours. And Annyon...the work he's become a part of..." She gulped and looked away. "We won't find safety, not if we're going to be unsealed."

I stared into her eyes, searching her for doubt. "Is that an *if*?"

She didn't flinch. "Not for me."

———

"As legitimized citizens, Americans will enjoy the benefits of public services such as police, schools, and healthcare. Added benefits will include free transportation, generous distribution rations, and public power without charge. All citizens will be provided..."

I rubbed my forehead and glanced over to Eliza. Her jaw moved in the way it did when she was annoyed, but her eyes remained steady on the screen. Economics 101. Ugh.

Ms. Sheffort continued her propaganda-laced lecture from the monitor up front. I drew a long breath and tried to keep my mind from wandering. The Progressives had won the presidency, and the next election was still three years away. Seemed a little soon to start pushing their rosy promises in our face. Early and often—that was the game, I guessed. Apparently they were good at it.

"Today we'll see how that comes together." Sheffort stopped, tapped on her digital Smart Board to open a document, and then smiled to her real-live students in the state center. Her eyes lifted to the camera, and she held her grin as if we actually mattered out here in the sticks. "Taxes. We don't like to discuss them, but they're necessary. The good news is, however, that the financial burden has been lifted by the Citizen Recharacterization Act. All *Americans* have been relieved by the careful planning and good graces of the PRP. We'll see how as we work through this assignment."

Taxes? Could we do anything more uninteresting? I glanced again at Eliza. She had centered her tab on her desk and tapped on the Student Work icon. I looked back to my own tab. I hadn't even opened the Econ application yet. Oh well. I was there. I might as well participate.

The assignment bloomed on my screen, a government form waiting to be filled in.

"First task..." Ms. Sheffort said.

I looked back to the large screen. Her Smart Board boasted the same form.

"...be sure to check the correct box under political affiliate."

Wait. That was the first task? Not fill in your name, be sure your social security number was correct?

I looked over to Eliza's screen. She'd already done all of that, and also checked her political-affiliate box. The form expanded, asking for all of her financial information.

Bringing my attention back to my own tab, I stared at the cursor as it blinked in the blank space for my name. Braxton M. Luther. I continued to fill out the required information, and then my finger hovered over the political-affiliate boxes. Progressive Reform Party. Traditionalist. What would happen...

As if acting in rebellion, my finger tapped on the PRP box. The form that opened was very different from Eliza's. Only my job and number of household members were required. I made up a career—structural engineer—and typed in the number 3 for the household. Boom. Done.

Congratulations, Citizen. Your information is being recorded. Please stand by for your healthcare voucher and equalization supplement quota numbers. Rest easy knowing your country has provided you with life, liberty, and happiness.

What was that? I sat up and leaned over to Eliza's desk. "Did you get this?" I whispered as I tipped my tab in her direction.

She turned her head toward my work. "No." Her gaze moved from the screen to my face. "What did you do?"

My chest hardened, and I swallowed. "Nothing. Why are you looking at me like that?"

She stared at me as if I'd just blurted out that she'd wet her pants at a school play when she was eight—which was her most embarrassing secret.

Her shoulders started to wilt. "Which box did you check?"

I licked my lips, but that didn't help the drought that seemed to have suddenly overtaken them. Swallowing didn't work either, as the drought spread rapidly down my throat. "I just wanted to see what would happen." I frowned. There was nothing wrong with that. "It's just an assignment, Liza."

"Hey, PK, let me see your tab." Tristan Melzner, one of my former teammates, hunkered over my shoulder.

I slid my tab over Eliza's. "Why?" My scowl deepened—I could feel my eyebrows almost touching.

Tristan shoved my shoulder back, giving himself a clear view of my assignment. His eyes scanned the screen, and then a satisfied, mocking kind of smile tipped the corners of his mouth. "Got something right for a change." He snorted a chuckle. "Maybe things will start looking up for the li'l Luther."

My grip tightened on the two tabs in my hands. "Didn't know I needed your approval, Melzner. Or maybe you just needed help reading the big words?"

His eyes narrowed. "Watch it, PK. Our eyes see everything."

What did that mean?

I slid a look over to Eliza. She kept her head down, but she winced like she could vomit. How had things gotten so twisted? One little box on a stupid form could change my social status? What else could it change?

Tristan stalked away, off to pester some other wayward citizen. I shuffled Eliza's tab to the top.

Be advised that you have willfully rejected the benefits of a Citizen. Please stand by for your tax bracket calculation...

The loading bar rolled for two more seconds, and then a number with a dollar sign flashed on the screen. Crikey. My heart actually stopped, I thought. Eliza would owe more in taxes than my father made in a year.

Payments will be calculated and deducted from your paychecks.

Uh, that would be every last dollar. I forced air into my chest. "What did you put as a career?"

"Administrative assistant." Eliza's pale face held mine with a grave message.

That was what my mother did. That was how she supplemented my father's preacher paycheck.

"How could they demand that much money from someone who doesn't even take home that amount?"

A chair screeched across the floor on the other side of the room, ripping our attention from our tabs.

"Got one," Tristan bellowed.

"Hey, that's my tab."

It was a guy I didn't ever talk to. He ran with the musical, artsy group—not my crowd. Well, Eliza didn't really qualify as a crowd, but the kid wasn't an athlete, so I didn't know him.

"All's fair in a citizens' search." Tristan had three other football players flanking his sides by then. "You didn't follow instructions, Song Bird. Pretty easy, even for a story-loving, heaven-seeking churchy like you. *Be sure to mark the correct box.* Didn't you hear Ms. Sheffort?"

The boy stood and grabbed for his tab. "I thought this was a free country."

"Free for citizens." Tristan grabbed the kid's jaw, lifting it up and to the side to expose his neck. "Which by the looks of things, you're not." He shoved him back into his chair and then crossed his dark well-muscled arms. "Who is this guy?"

"Kipper Elliot." One of the other boys answered. "Attends the little church on the edge of town. In the poverty section. Uncloaked."

Uncloaked? What was that?

Tristan smirked. "Clearly. Family?"

"All Uncloaked."

"Noted." He leaned over Kipper, who cowered like he expected a blow. "Fix it, boy. You're in our sights."

Kipper didn't respond. I detected a tremble in the boy's hands, but he held a strong gaze. A gaze that seemed somehow familiar in nature. I glanced to Eliza. She was biting her lip as she kept her eyes fixed on Kipper. My view widened, encompassing both of them. His eyes darted to her, and she nodded ever so slightly.

Wait. What just happened? My chest expanded with a fierceness I hadn't anticipated. I zeroed back in on Eliza, wanting to take her by the arm and pull her to my side. What was this guy doing, looking to Liza for strength? She didn't have any to spare. *And she's mine.*

Wasn't she?

"What do you expect me to say?" Kipper's weak voice ripped me out of my Braxtonian-centered universe.

Tristan still hovered over the guy. "Show us a sign of loyalty."

"What do you want?"

"I think you'll find life much easier if you comply." Tristan tapped Kipper's tab. "Try it. See what happens when you check the correct box."

My attention dropped to my own tab. *The correct box.* Not

the right box—as in what is true of you, but the correct box—as in PC.

Congratulations, Citizen.

The words burned in my vision.

Check a box. Get on with your life.

My own voice echoed in my ears. Was it really that easy? We were living like impoverished beggars at the Knights' house, and it could have been avoided by checking the correct box?

"I won't." Kipper's meek voice beckoned my attention again.

The air seemed to turn cold and hard. Eliza pulled in a long breath and held it. I scowled, first at her and then at Kipper. Tristan looked to his right and then to his left. The bulky guys flanking him returned his glance with smirks.

He smacked Kipper on the back of his head, sending the kid's face toward the desk. "It's your funeral."

I assumed that was figurative. Couldn't be anything but, despite the zinging sense of fear rising in my chest. Not in this country.

CHAPTER SIX

Tristan's voice nagged me the rest of the day. So did Eliza's apparent connection with Kipper. How dare she have other *guy* friends? Crikey. There was that ego vortex thing again.

I caught up with her at the end of the day as she shrugged into her heavy coat. "Let's walk home," I said, leaning over her shoulder.

She looked at me for two heartbeats, her eyebrows quirking inward. "Okay..."

No arguments, no lectures—despite the fact that the temperature had hovered around twenty degrees all day, and the sun would bid us good night in about an hour. The rock in my chest loosened a little. Still my girl.

She set her tab in her locker and flashed the code-card over the lock. I took her lunch bag and shoved it into my pack so her hands would be free to poke into her pockets once we were outside. Side by side, we walked through the halls without a word.

The air bit at my nose as the humid chill seeped through

my heavy coat, sinking all the way to my bones. We had a three-mile trek ahead of us—two and a half if we cut through the woods. Me and my great ideas. But I needed to sort some things out in private.

We passed under the skeleton of hickory trees, our breaths coming out in puffy clouds before I spoke. "Did you know about the tax brackets?"

Eliza shrugged. "I knew they'd changed. I told you the taxes hit us hard."

"I thought you were talking about pew taxes."

Her chin turned up toward me. "Your dad won't let anyone pay those. We give more to the church, but I'm sure it doesn't cover the whole amount."

A big puff of air wisped from my nose. "How do you know about all this stuff?"

Eliza's footsteps slowed as she focused on me. I stopped and held her gaze while I wondered why her eyes held pity.

She turned to face me. "I wish you'd try talking to your parents."

That was where her sympathy came from? "Can't," I snapped. "They meet by appointment only. Or crisis. I don't have either."

"You used to hang with your dad."

"I used to like football too." I looked away, trying to tamp down my frustration. "Why are we talking about this anyway?"

She shrugged, but her expression didn't lose the etching of concern. "Because that's how I know about this stuff. From my parents. We've talked about it. About why this is happening, about what may happen and how we should respond. Dad says it's better to prepare in the light for what may come in the dark."

I growled. More goody-goody, be-ready-for-the-end stuff. I'd never have guessed the Knights to be preppers. "Do you have stuff stashed away in your basement?" I mocked.

"What?" She pulled back as her face scrunched up.

"You know. A year's supply of toilet paper. Enough dehydrated food to last until Judgment Day."

Eliza's shoulders dropped, and her mouth screwed up to one side. Irritation actually looked cute on her. Better than panic. I grinned.

"Stop it, Braxton." She shoved at my arm.

Chuckling, I caught her hand and held it against the spot she'd pushed, happy that she was still mine. And then the look that had passed between her and Kipper replayed in my mind. My smile dropped.

"What's the deal with you and Kipper Elliot?"

She pulled her hand away, and her face went all confused again. "Can *you* even keep pace with your random brain?"

"Don't avoid the question."

"I'm not." She crossed her arms. "I'd answer if I understood what you're talking about."

"I saw *the look*."

"The look?" She snorted. "You saw him looking at me?"

I shoved my hands into my coat pockets, taking a small step toward her. "I saw you looking at each other, when Tristan had him by the neck. It wasn't just any old look."

"Crikey."

She mocked my Australian slang, which I'd picked up in subtle rebellion against my father. He quit barking at me to stop using it over a year ago, but I kept it in my vocabulary mostly out of habit—and a little bit because I knew it still irritated him.

Eliza shook her head, and her eyes rolled. "Of all the things you could worry about, that's what you're stuck on?"

What had my mouth gotten me into? It was one thing to like a girl, way different to actually tell her. Especially when she was the girl you spent all your time with—almost literally. What happened when she said she didn't feel that way about me? I wasn't prepared for the *let's just be friends* spiel from Eliza. Rejection from her would be worse than my fa—

Crikey. Where was that going? Worse than being cut from the football team. Yeah. Worse than that.

"I'm not stuck on anything." I huffed. "I didn't ` ow you knew the guy, that's all."

Eliza pinned me with her intense gaze, almost as if she knew what I was thinking. Her expression softened. "He was on the premed track before the retesting. We had classes together. His dad's blue collar, and they live across town, but he was able to transfer schools when he tested into the Career Track, and somehow his family managed the education fees." Her eyes drifted away from me.

Eliza's life had changed, and so had Kipper's. They would never get into med school since they'd been kicked out of Career Track. College, maybe, but she'd never be able to pursue her ambitions, and neither would Kipper. I knew what that punch in the gut felt like.

I looked to the ground. "He's not sealed."

"No." She raised her eyes to me. "There are a few of us left."

Be strong. Stand with us.

I wanted to assure her, to affirm the plea I could read in her eyes, but Tristan's mocking voice ripped through my mind, confusing my resolve.

It's your funeral.

Why would I choose misery when a simple checkmark in a box could restore all that we had lost?

Because it's the right thing to do. Eliza's voice spoke—in my head. Weird. Was telepathy a real thing? Nah. Just something she would say. She was always right too.

I sighed. "Do you think he's going to be okay?"

She seemed to freeze. Surprise brushed over her eyes, and then...pride. "What do you think?"

With rapid-fire clarity, scenes scrolled through my memory. Practice. Being cut. The rally.

Uncloaked. As in, unsafe.

Had it really come to that? My palm went to my neck, which was swathed by my winter coat. My naked, unsealed neck. Up to that point, Eliza and I hadn't been called out publicly about our noncitizen status—if you didn't count Coach. But what happened when someone was singled out, warned, and they still ignored the demand?

What would happen to Kipper?

I looked back to the school. Only a few students milled around, no one I recognized. Suddenly an image of Kipper thrust into my imagination. Tristan had ahold of his neck, but they weren't in a classroom. Kipper was pinned against something large and metal. A flashback, but not really. A flashforward? Panic beat like a drum against my throat.

"I think he might be in trouble." I looked to Eliza again.

She nodded, her eyes darkening. "I think maybe you're right. What should we do?"

I rubbed my chin. This reaction—terror—was probably an overreaction. He'd be fine.

My pulse throbbed harder. I gulped. "Do you know where he lives?"

Pursing her lips, she shook her head. "Just across town in the poverty section. That's all I know."

Shoulders drooped, I blew out a gust of air and looked back to the school. Relief? No. Should have been. I didn't want mixed up with that guy. My own troubles were already heaping. I didn't need to take on Kipper's too. But something in my gut compelled me to action, which was outside of my normal scope.

I could talk to my father about it. He'd know how to find Kipper's family, know what to do. But that would require... talking to my father. Once again, outside of my scope, and I wasn't going to stretch that far for this Kipper kid.

"Elliot, right?" I glanced back to Eliza. "His last name is Elliot?"

"Yes."

I took one more long breath. *Here goes...my first attempt at nobility.* "We could go to Main—to the Juice Shop. They have a digital census there. Maybe we can find out more."

Eliza smiled. Not the full, happy kind, but the *I'm glad to be your friend* kind.

Affirmation for my first wobbly step into selflessness. Taking her by the elbow, we set off together for Main Street.

———

We found the Elliots on the census, which had been created before my lifetime. Something about the Bloody Faith Conflict and deportations and things that I didn't think mattered much anymore. The Elliots' house was over six miles away. The winter sun had already started to fade. I stared at the screen with Eliza by my side, wondering what to do. Actually, I knew what to do: nothing. We couldn't do anything right then. But that didn't settle in my stomach too well.

"Now what?" I looked at her.

Uncertainty played in her eyes. She'd been thinking the same thoughts. Feeling the same uneasy feeling. "Your dad would know."

Great. The last resort, and we were there already. I did one more mental search for another solution.

Commotion outside the Juice Shop's window snagged my concentration. A black van crawled down Main Street with green-jacketed boys marching on either side, like a parade. People stopped on the wide sidewalks outside of the shops, staring. Some shouted.

"Reform!" A tall, burly man shook his fist in the air.

The marching boys looked straight ahead. Most smirked.

I followed with my eyes as the van continued its slow procession toward the LiteRail. Silent alarms jarred my brain, which compelled me to follow that vehicle.

"Stay here," I mumbled. I didn't wait to see if she would.

Without being too conspicuous, I hurried after the impromptu parade until it stopped at the far corner of the Lite-Rail station. The boys scurried to the cab, each pulling something out of the front passenger door. Sticks. No...clubs. The hair on my neck poked at my coat.

One boy, large and familiar, opened the back of the van. Reaching inside, he yanked, and a person stumbled from the back. A woman with oatmeal-colored hair and wearing a thin, worn-out coat not warm enough for the bite of our humid winters. She was about my mother's age. Another green-coated boy pulled out a second passenger.

Kipper Elliot.

Breathing suddenly felt impossible. What were they doing with Kipper?

Two more people were tugged from the back of the van. A girl about Hannah's age and a man whose thin hair waved helplessly in the cold winter breeze.

Kipper's family.

The big familiar kid swung his club, landing a blow in the man's gut.

"This is what your god can do?"

I knew that bellowing voice.

"Can he protect you, Preacher?"

He doubled his fist and plowed it into the man's face. "Yield, fool!"

Kipper's father stumbled, and Mrs. Elliot caught him. He struggled to stand upright again, and Kipper stepped in front of him. "No."

Another bully backhanded Kipper. "You will. Here or there. You will reform."

Kipper wobbled, and his mother cried out.

"Shut up, woman." The big one, who seemed to be in charge, raised his stick over her. "I'd rather not hit a female. Even if she is a dirty faith vermin."

She curled her arm around her daughter and huddled over her. "Please don't."

"Then yield!"

Silence. The woman muffled a sob, but none of the captives spoke.

Two large puffs of white floated in my face—I was breathing like I'd been running wind sprints. My rib cage actually hurt as my heart beat hard against it.

"Move!" the bellower jabbed Kipper in the back.

Surrounded by ruffians, the Elliots staggered toward a lone

LiteRail car. I repositioned myself, careful to stay out of sight while I watched.

"All aboard." The boy sneered.

First Kipper's sister, then his mother and father, and finally Kipper mounted the two steps onto the car. The big guy in green snagged Kipper by the collar and ripped him back to the ground. With a flick of his wrist, he spun Kipper to face him and then grabbed his neck, shoving him up against the metal LiteRail car.

"Look around, Bible Boy." The club-holding boy leaned close but kept his loud, mocking tone turned up. "This is the last time you'll see this life." He pulled Kipper forward and then slammed his head against the side of the car. With a grunt, Kipper slumped down, and two other boys took him by the shoulders and threw him into the car.

I shut my eyes and tried not to hyperventilate.

A hand tugged me backward. My eyes flew open as I whipped around, my fists doubled.

"It's okay," Eliza whispered. "It's just me."

"What are you doing?" I hissed. "I told you to stay at the Juice Shop. They might see you!"

Tears snuck past her eyelids, and she looked beyond me. "Where are they going?"

Craning my neck, I caught a final glimpse of the Elliots as the LiteRail pulled away. I had no idea where they were going, but I was certain they wouldn't be coming back.

A spasm clenched my stomach, and I almost lost whatever was left of my lunch. What had I just seen?

CHAPTER SEVEN

NOTICE OF EVICTION.

I didn't have to read the orange paper posted on our front door to know what it was, but I couldn't steer my eyes away from it. How could they kick us out of our home?

For failure to comply with the ordered civil action, the owners of 272 Mulberry Lane are hereby notified that this property and all of its contents have now reverted to the possession of the US government.

Wait. The US government? I thought foreclosures defaulted to the bank. And what civil action? Make your payments. Keep your house. That was how this whole deal worked.

I don't know why I tried to put logic to it. Nothing about anything in our life made sense anymore. Scenes from last week, from the Elliots' departure, haunted me. No one spoke of it, but the edge in the air couldn't be denied. Who would be next?

I didn't want to know the answer. Every time I looked at Eliza, I saw her unsealed neck and struggled for a steady breath. Facing reality had become too terrifying, so making sense of the chaos seemed like the better option.

Besides, it wasn't hard to believe that my parents had defaulted on a house loan, not with the change in taxes. As it was, house repossession was fairly common.

I swallowed, turning to my father. "How long have you not paid the mortgage?" I didn't mean to carry accusation in my voice. When it came to stuff between my father and me though, indictment just came naturally.

"We didn't have to." He snatched the notice and smashed it into a ball. "We've owned it for two years, free and clear."

He had to be kidding. On a preacher's salary? In this economic slump? Didn't seem likely that he'd lie to me though. "This doesn't make any sense. How can they take our house if we own it?"

"Because I wasn't compliant."

Yeah, I got that. Right there, from the notice. "About what?"

My father turned tired, smoldering eyes on me. "Why aren't you playing football, son?"

My stare fell to my shoes.

"I know about the shirt, Braxton." Challenge radiated from his intense expression. "I know about Coach cutting you. Why do you think he did it?"

Of course I knew the truth—just like I had when Eliza and I had this same confrontation. But it didn't seem possible. I had to have missed something along the way.

Rolling my shoulders back, I glared. "Because I'm not you. Or Jamis. Or Annyon." Like my father needed a fight at that moment. But there was something in me I couldn't shut down. I had to prove to my father that I wasn't afraid of him—even if I was. Because then maybe I wouldn't be his bean-pole afterthought son anymore. "I wasn't first-string material, wasn't worth the uniform or the space I took up riding the bench. Why do you care, anyway? You only made it to two games last year."

Father looked away, the hardness on his face dissolving into something pathetic. His gaze fell to a spot on the ground where the snow had piled deep. With a slow exhale, his chest caved inward like...like he was defeated.

I'd defeated him.

It felt sickening. Weird. I'd spent the last four years trying to best my father. Now I'd done it, and I wanted to vomit.

"I'm sorry, Braxton," he whispered.

I could see his soul through his exhausted, downcast posture. A soul broken. Pummeled by failure. The church was folding, he'd lost our home, and I'd just kicked him in the gut.

He reached for the door and moved through the entry, his feet barely leaving the ground as he shuffled. My father—the football star, the famous preacher, the invincible man—was old. A vice gripped inside my chest, crushing the region where my heart was supposed to be.

I followed him with my face directed to the floor. I hated shame. Hated. It. Especially when it came as a result of something said between my father and me. Pulling my spine straight, I set my jaw hard.

My resolve not to buckle under guilt hit a wall as I walked through the door. Crikey. Our place had been ransacked. Broken chairs littered the dining room. My mother's piano had been smashed—judging by the deep pockmarks in the crafted wood, someone had taken a sledgehammer to it. Picture frames lay helter skelter on the floor, the glass shattered. Even the walls proclaimed vengeance—the same deep holes on the piano punctured the drywall, and smaller divots scarred the paint where the picture frames had been thrown.

Father's breath released in a low, barely audible groan. His hand grazed the piano—mother's inheritance from her grandmother—and he leaned against it while his head dropped forward.

My chin quivered, but I ground my teeth, jamming pity down deep enough to be ignored. He deserved this—he could have complied with whatever they wanted him to do. He didn't always have to be so dang stubborn. Now, finally, he could see he was not the invincible Patrick Luther he'd always thought he'd been.

What was it they wanted him to do?

"Is this because of the taxes?" The ice in my voice seemed cruel, but I refused to feel bad.

"No." Father pulled the piano bench out, which ironically still sat in perfect condition under the smashed keys. Slumping onto it, he looked like a marionette whose strings had been cut off. "It's because I didn't fill out the forms."

"What forms?"

He raised his eyes to me, and life began to return. "Attendance forms." His voice bit both words, disdain for the Party still boiling hot. Valor snuck back into his posture. He wasn't sorry for his noncompliance. Not sorry at all.

I should be proud of him, because he was strong enough to take the blows without regretting his principles. Except his principles had just made us homeless. Despicable ideology.

"Why?" I snapped.

His shoulders pulled back, and the great imposing football preacher returned. "Because it's wrong. I'm not reporting to the government who is attending church." Conviction smoldered in his eyes, setting his tone aflame. "Do you know why they want to know, Braxton? Why they're keeping track?"

My confidence evaporated, even though my irritation continued to climb. "Why?"

You know how every lame Christian movie about rebellious teenagers always had the kid snapping, sounding like some kind of juvenile delinquent snot? Yeah. That was how I sounded. I cringed, despising my immaturity.

With an unwavering gaze, Father wordlessly communicated some kind of grave prophecy before he spoke. "Because they're trying to identify the Cloaked."

A shiver rippled down my spine. Whispers had rustled in the halls of our school about the Cloaked. People who had taken the oath, received the Citizen's Seal, but weren't loyal to the Party. *They will be found, cut out, and made to be an example.*

What would be their example?

But then again, why would my father protect them? He preached faithfulness, even if it meant *inconvenience.* Losing one's house fell under that category, I supposed. Why would Father guard those who had taken on the symbol of the ungodded? The Cloaked still sat in their comfortable homes, ate real food. Their kids were still welcomed in the school, playing sports, maintaining their positions in the Career Track. They were neither faithful nor deserving.

Uncloaked. Understanding blitzed in between my ears. They were the people who refused the seal. The outright defiant. They were us. What would happen to the Uncloaked? The Elliot scene reemerged, and my lungs suddenly felt as though they were collapsing.

Father was covering the Cloaked, but the Uncloaked—our fate was much worse. What was this double standard that he maintained? *We* must sacrifice to be faithful, and yet he'd protect those who did not?

Heat flashed through my body.

"We lost our home for *them*?" I picked up a frame and flung it across the room. "Do you know what kids say about me and Eliza at school? Do you know what happened to—"

I stopped short. I still couldn't talk about Kipper. The Eliza jab was enough. Her honor was something that should be upheld. Even Father would agree.

"The situation is not that unusual, Braxton. Many families share a home these days. And anyway, God knows the truth."

I blew out a hot breath. "Yes. He does," I shouted. "So why are we refusing the seal when we could take it to be compliant, knowing that God knows what is true in our hearts?"

His stare smoldered. "It's not the same."

"Why?"

Silence penetrated my selfishness, but I refused to crumple under the conviction. I hated that he could stare other people into submission. I wouldn't be like those people. I stretched straight, from my feet to the top of my head, returning his silent demand for surrender.

"You know why." He barely moved his mouth as his low voice descended on me.

A quiet voice did *not* always turn away wrath. Especially when it was steeped with disappointment.

Surely my brothers, if they had been here and not off living their own successful grown-up lives, would have entered the house in respectful silence, taken up a broom or gone to pack what was necessary, and commiserated with my father as a good son ought to. I was *not* one of them. Never had been.

I pivoted, kicked an overturned lamp out of my path, and stomped toward the door.

"Braxton." Father's coarse whisper prickled in my ears.

I paused, refusing to look back to him.

"Your fight is not with me, son."

Maybe so, but he was there. And he was the reason we didn't have a home. Seemed cause enough to stay mad—at him and at his stupid church.

———

My tennis shoes hit the front porch before the muzzle of an automatic weapon jabbed me in the chest. Frozen to the spot, my veins pulsed with ice.

"What are you doing here, boy?"

My eyes jumped to the man who had pushed the gun's barrel into my chest. Well, barely a man—he was maybe five years older than me. He wore heavy khaki pants and a uniformed jacket, green, with the circle emblem of the Progressive Party embroidered on the left shoulder.

"I—"

"Shut up." He raised the end of his gun so it stared me in the face.

I snapped my mouth closed. A leer crept over his mouth as he swayed his weapon in small circles in front of my head. Holding my breath, I matched his long look.

The cold metal of the gun grazed over my cheek and then slid to my chin. With a jerk, he forced my head to the side, giving him full exposure to my neck.

"No seal." He used the gun to jerk my face back to him.

I swallowed. "Is that a crime?"

His eyebrow quirked. "Not yet." The gun hung in my face for two more agonizing breaths. "Get out of here, kid. Get yourself sealed, before my trigger finger forgets that you're a minor."

He pulled the gun from my face and then used it to shove me to the side. I tripped down the stairs as the guy, along with two other uniformed man-boys, entered our house.

I looked around the front yard for more armed Party officials. Only the icy roads and snow-laden trees met my inspection. Stepping carefully, I slid close to the deck railing on our front porch, where I could see through the front window.

"You!" The leader barked from just inside the door. "What are you doing here?"

My father stood straight, his hands held up, palms flat against the frigid winter air. "I was coming to get a few things." He kept his eyes on the armed guard. "This is—was my house."

The muzzle of the gun flew across the air, landing a hard blow along my father's jaw. He stumbled to the side.

"This property belongs to the PRP." The gunman stepped closer, reinserting his weapon in my father's face. "You're trespassing."

"Please, we just need—"

This time the butt of the gun smashed against the side of his head. Blood trickled from behind his ear. Father tripped back, hitting the demolished piano, and then crumpled to the floor.

I bit my tongue as the rest of my body went painfully numb. Squeezing my eyes shut, I tried to erase the imprint of my father's bloody face from my mind.

"Get him. These people need to know what defiance will cost."

Boots hammered against the floorboards, and then a grunt echoed from the house. They were coming. I couldn't be here. Crouching below the floor line of the raised deck, I scurried to the corner of the house and ducked around the side.

A black van crept forward from behind a stand of hickory trees at the corner of our street as they drug my unconscious father out, letting his legs bounce down the two front steps and over the snow.

I waited until I could no longer hear the rumbling engine of their black van before I took off at a sprint. Rounding the back of our house, I bolted to the creek and then followed it north until I found our tree.

A twig snapped across the creek. I jumped and spun around, expecting to see another uniform.

Hannah stared at me, her arms full of dead twigs.

"What are you doing out here?" I took three quick steps and then leapt across the width of frozen water. "Come on. We need to go inside."

Her face scrunched. "Why? I'm just getting kindling sticks."

I tugged on her arm. "It's not safe."

She didn't argue, because I didn't give her a chance. With me nearly dragging her, we ran across the creek and to the Knights' backyard. Even then I didn't stop my pumping legs and wouldn't let Hannah slow up either. I shoved through the back door, and we tumbled into the Knights' living room.

Burning hickory filled my nostrils, and the warmth of a fire enveloped my exposed cheeks. I didn't let myself enjoy it. "Shut the curtains."

Eliza, who had been stretched out on her stomach in front of the fire, looked up from her book. Our mothers also stopped —mine from some kind of paperwork I'd never thought to ask about, and hers from chopping root vegetables at the table in the kitchen across the room.

"What's going on?" Mrs. Knight looked to Hannah, who raised her eyebrows.

"Braxton's being weird," Hannah said.

Eliza sat up, her face marked with a cautious question.

My mother stood from her chair and stepped toward me. "Where's your father?"

All eyes glued to my face, waiting in a silence that rippled gooseflesh on my arms.

"They took him." My voice quivered.

My focus landed on Mother first, whose horror quickly dissolved into a silent trail of tears, and then shifted to Eliza. Her wide, terrified eyes spoke to me from across the room.

It's our turn.

CHAPTER EIGHT

Why didn't they come after all of us, like they had the Elliots?

I couldn't formulate an answer. But finding out what happened to my father took priority over the whys I couldn't explain.

The LiteRail hadn't sent a late car westbound after dark the night he'd been taken. We asked the few people we still trusted—the ones who still snuck to Sunday services—careful to disguise our motive. That left only one option, if we were getting a straight story. My father was being held somewhere in town. I wouldn't allow any other possibilities in my mind.

It took a week to find out where he was, and even then, it was only by luck. We risked going to the police, because my father had worked with them so often over the past seven years. Part of the preacher job. Mother and I believed the chief would remember my father's help and kindness, which, hopefully, would overrule the new social order. Maybe it would have, but Chief Sanders wasn't there.

All local government and law enforcement had been

replaced by PRP-appointed officials. They denied his arrest—because it wasn't really an arrest. I described the uniform jacket to the police official Mother and I were forced to talk to. He tipped a half a nod.

"That is the coat of the Jackals, young man." The officer's short, narrow mustache twitched. "But they are not armed. They're a group of brave young men who have set aside the comforts of home and family to train for the defense of the United States."

"Don't we have an army for that?"

My mother frowned at my impertinence. I couldn't help it. The man had *liar, liar* written all over his face. The men who had taken my father had most definitely been armed, and if they were the Jackals, then this PRP official knew more than he was telling us.

The man smiled. "We can never have enough insurance. Once our new way of life is established, we will be the envy of nations. That is a precarious position, and one we will be ready to defend when it comes time."

An answer that provoked more questions. I tipped my head as if I were actually interested. "And exactly who do you expect to fight?"

"Braxton." Mother eyed me the way she always did when my mouth had embarrassed her.

"No worries." A laugh shook the man's chest. "A spirited young man, aren't you? Well, the Jackals need your kind. You'd be welcomed in their ranks."

I glared into his amused eyes. "I'm not sealed."

"A problem you should remedy." His smile remained plastered, but the laughter in his eyes narrowed into a deadly stare. "Soon."

A trickle of ice ran down my spine, but I refused to cower. "Where's my father?"

"Is he sealed?"

My mouth snapped shut. Silence swirled around us like a vine of evil smothering every scrap of life in its path.

"I see." He spoke in a cool tone. "Noncitizens are not protected by the government. I am not obligated to help you." He turned as if to leave but stopped after a single step and set a dark look on me. "Something, perhaps, you should consider."

My chest trembled, and heat burned my ears as my mother pulled me away. We left the courthouse—the building that housed the local police and the sheriff's department, and more recently, where the PRP officials had set up their offices. I pounded down the three steps and then paused on the sidewalk running the length of downtown.

The prison had been built next to the courthouse, but visiting an inmate required a pass. It seemed unlikely, anyway, that my father would be in there—in government housing where prisoners were fed three times a day, allowed hot showers, and given a decent bed. Not the place they would throw a noncitizen—the Uncloaked —since they were not the responsibility of the US government.

I scanned the buildings towering over Main Street. Two were abandoned—one had been a museum, but nobody went to those anymore. It closed its doors over thirty years ago. The other had been a bookstore. The cyber age had buried it fifty years past.

Though empty, I doubted my father would be in either. Here in the heart of downtown, the buildings were too exposed to people. If the Jackals were hiding a kidnapped man, they wouldn't do it on Main Street.

A high-pitched whistle blared through the cold air. The

LiteRail was nearing the depot south of town. Its tracks had been laid overtop of the old railroad, laying to rest for good the diesel dinosaur. But across from the rails and beyond the convenience-goods storefronts lining the depot area, an old factory rested in its forsaken loneliness. No one ever went that way. There wasn't a reason to go past the LiteRail—all life in town radiated north of that point.

I grabbed Mother's elbow, pulling her down the sidewalk. We crossed the street and continued east until we came to an alley.

Tugging her into the abandoned way, I whispered, "I know where he is."

She halted in midstride. "Where?"

I backpedaled two steps to stay with her. "The old hose factory."

Her frown looked more like dread than doubt. The factory had been a mausoleum of outdated technology and goods all my life. More than once it'd been the scene of unthinkable brutality. It housed vagabonds, black-market criminals, and druggies.

And now my father. I was certain.

———

Most of the windows had been shattered—the ancient glass hadn't been treated to withstand any sort of impact, and rocks had found their way from the palms of mischievous hands to the panes inlaid in fiberglass frames.

The old railroad had utilized the loading dock once upon a time—back when trains transported goods more than people and farmers still watered with hoses dangling from overhead pivots. We followed the iron tracks to the covered dock. Rust had eaten through most of the metal siding, and the red of its presence spread over the rest of the dingy-yellow sheet like leprosy. It creaked against the force of wind, which had picked up once we left the microclimate established by the rise of buildings in town.

Ignoring the thick corroded chains that wrapped the iron double doors, I pulled on the frost-laden handle. The door didn't budge.

My eyes traveled the length of the building—two football fields, at least. Half as wide, and three stories tall. My father could be anywhere in the dilapidated dungeon. The steel siding, though as discolored as the docking bay, was solid all the way to the corner, and the windows were all a story above my head.

"We should try the front," Mother said. Her eyes had followed mine, and she pulled at my arm as she stepped toward the nearest corner.

I stopped her, pulling her back. "What if the Jackals are in front? What if they've got guards?"

"We can't let him die in there."

No, we couldn't. Assuming he wasn't already dead. But I couldn't let my mother walk into a hive, either.

"I'll go alone." I dragged her back to the loading doors. "I can sneak around. I won't be as noticeable on my own."

Mother bit her lip, tears shining her eyes. "What happens if I lose you both?"

"You won't." I scowled, hating that her emotion spiked fear inside of me. "I'll be back. I promise." I walked away, hopping off the two-foot drop from the loading dock to the snowy ground.

"Braxton—"

"Just stay put." I didn't turn to see her. My stomach quivered enough. I didn't need her terror to cripple my sudden burst of courage.

Scrambling to form a plan, I ordered my heart to stop pumping fear through my veins. As the memory of the cold muzzle of an automatic weapon rippled gooseflesh over my neck, my heart disobeyed. Terror pulsed through my whole body.

What would I find on the other side of the building? Armed guards on the lookout for feeble rescue attempts? If I got past them by some stroke of miraculous intervention, where would I find my father? The bowels of this relic were large. Who knew what was on the inside.

I stopped at the corner of the building, flattening myself against the icy metal siding. This was it—I had to do this. I balled my fist as one last tremble shook my body.

Fear is not my friend. I forced my back straight as I clenched my jaw. *I will not be afraid.* I refused to live in fear—of anything. They would not rob me of courage. Guns or no guns, I would not bow to their intimidation.

I swallowed, feeling my face set in hard determination. Yes. This is me. And I will do what I have set out to do.

I peeked around the corner to inspect what I would face. The front entrance stood lonely; deserted just as the rest of the building. My shoulders dropped as my lungs emptied. Disappointment. Not relief. No guards meant my father probably wasn't there—that I'd been wrong. If he wasn't there, then I had no idea where he was.

No, I had an idea. A visual of the final glimpse I'd had of Kipper Elliot flashed through my mind. I was certain they wouldn't come back from that train ride. My father could...

Mother would be devastated. I couldn't give up yet.

Still pressed against the building, I stepped around the

corner, clinging to a small hope that I'd see something that would indicate life. As I moved to the doors, nothing surfaced. Reaching the entrance, I sagged one shoulder against the steel.

Wait. There was something in the snow in front of the door. Almost indiscernible, but a breeze swept against the icy snow on the ground and rumpled a small, folded paper.

The bite of the snow made my already-cold fingers ache as I reached for the note. Folded in quarters, the white page was only a small slip of paper. The handwriting hit my eyes after I tugged it open, and my heart punched my rib cage. Father's.

Conviction over comfort.

Was that intended for me?

I stood straight, jamming some kind of guilt-and-anger cocktail deep into my gut, and tugged on the handle. It gave. I pulled harder, determined to open the heavy door. Hinges, old and rusted, moaned against my disturbance. I cringed. When I had enough space cracked, I slipped through and flattened myself against the wall in the darkness of the shadows.

The door creaked itself closed, and the latch echoed after it caught. I waited, barely controlling my breathing so that I would not sound like a dog panting for air after a chase. Shadows became more defined as my eyes slowly adjusted to the gray interior. Slender shafts of sunlight angled through the darkness, let in by rusted breaches in the siding. The cold air smelled of damp dirt, rotted wood, and mold.

I stood on what had once been a solid concrete floor. Now it was cracked and heaved, creating a jumbled obstacle course —the job decay, time, and neglect were proficient in. This had been the manufacturing floor. Smashed machinery littered the corners of the large space, their jagged forms creating shadowy monsters left to watch over the eerie darkness.

Scanning every object, I forced my imagination into a

locked box so that it would not run interference. I had to do this. My vision followed the back wall, picking out the doors to the loading dock where my mother waited. I continued to scan the length of the wall until I saw a set of industrial stairs.

Bingo. My target.

I didn't dare traipse out into the open gloom. Any half-witted dummy who'd been set on guard duty would have heard the door open and shut and would be looking for a fool to wander into their crosshairs. My only chance was to stick to the shadows, which were heaviest against the walls.

Using my hands, I followed the siding at my back, ignoring the creepy gauze of spider's silk that entangled my fingers and brushed against my neck. My foot caught on a chunk of concrete that had been pushed up two inches above the floor line by years of freezing and then thawing. I caught myself with one hand before my face hit the cement, and I swallowed the grunt that nearly escaped from my mouth. I needed to watch more carefully where I stepped.

It seemed like night should be falling by the time I'd made it around the huge space to the stairway. I couldn't keep taking so much time. What if someone discovered my mother waiting in the back? What if she decided to follow me because I'd been gone so long?

The hardness fell over my face again. I would do this.

Looking up, I found the metal stairs led up to a catwalk that overlooked the manufacturing floor space on one side and a series of doors on the other. Offices, probably. The stairs turned and continued to the third floor, which was solid all the way from one end of the building to the other. Remembering the windows I'd seen from the outside, I decided to start on the third floor. If I were kidnapping someone, I'd keep them on the third floor—less likely to attempt a leaping escape.

The image of my father as I'd last seen him—bleeding and lying crumpled on the floor—flashed through my mind. He wouldn't be leaping anywhere. He may not even be conscious. Or alive.

My chest squeezed, and I banished the picture into the box where I'd imprisoned my imagination. Only helpful thoughts right now.

I placed my foot on the stairs and gave the structure one solid shake. It swayed a small bit but didn't groan. It'd handle me—I hoped. Surveying the upper catwalk, the parts that I could see, and finding nothing that set off alarms, I decided a swift ascent was my best option. Keeping to the balls of my feet, I took the stairs two at a time, thankful for the first time in my life that I did not carry the bulky frame of the typical Luther build.

One long hall stretched in front of me after I reached the third floor. Windows flanked the right side, three closed doors the left. I skipped the first. Who would put a prisoner there? I paused at the second. Maybe. But I could come back if the last proved empty. Checking behind me, I sneaked across the floor to the third. The handle gave under my hand with an easy turn, which I found discouraging, but I'd check anyway, just in case.

A new and sickening smell smacked against my face and slithered into my offended nostrils. Human waste, with the added undertones of prolific body odor and...and blood. Maybe death. My stomach kicked upward with a painful twist, and the taste of bile flooded my mouth. I tugged the neck of my shirt up over my nose and mouth and held it there with one hand while I scanned the room.

The windows had been covered over with black paper, but

sunlight still filtered through, allowing me to see the struggling movement of a human form against the far wall.

"Dad," I said under my hand and ran toward him.

Though I'd never really touched my father—we weren't the demonstrative, affectionate type—he felt smaller as I fumbled to help him sit up.

"Braxton—" His voice garbled weak and emotional. Nothing at all like the powerful preacher-man's bellow. "How..." The words cut off, as if he couldn't even manage one simple sentence.

"We're going." I pushed a shoulder under him, ignoring his pungent stench and the way his body recoiled with pain at my touch. Thankful for the dark, I didn't what to imagine what he looked like. "I need you to stand—you know I can't carry you."

He grunted a sound of protest. "Ties..."

Ties...ties...I sorted through reason to understand. Zip ties. I reached for my pocket knife. "Where?"

"Neck. Hands. Feet."

Neck? I moved from underneath his arm, which I'd been supporting, and fingered around his neck. Wiry hair prickled against my fingers as they searched for the strap that held him. A smooth band met my touch near his Adam's apple, a half-inch wide and a centimeter thick. I tried to slip my finger through, but it had been snugged down tight, leaving no space.

"How can you breathe?"

"Be still."

Was he giving me an answer or rebuking my questions? I ground my teeth. "Hold on. It'll probably hurt."

He craned his head back, stretching his neck. I worked my blade between his skin and the tie, hoping I wasn't catching his flesh. My father didn't make a sound, even when I yanked the knife to cut the cord.

"What was that attached to?"

His head dropped forward, and he drew a long, wheezy breath. "The wall. With another zip tie."

I pulled him forward and followed his arm from one shoulder down to his hands. They too had been secured tight, one tie around each hand, and one securing them tightly together, and another connected to a ring in the wall. I slipped the knife against one wrist to free first one hand and then another. After I had his feet, devoid of the shoes I'd last seen him with, unbound, I tugged him up. He followed, and I found myself surprised to discover that his bulk, though less than it had been, still overshadowed me.

"Come on. I know how to get out." Like there were multiple ways. I wondered if he'd scold my drama.

He followed in silence until we reached the door. I pulled his elbow, intending to drape his arm over my shoulders, but he tugged away and dropped to the floor.

"Dad, I'm serious." I yanked at his arm. "I really don't think I can get you down those stairs. You have to try."

He ignored me. Typical. My chest began to burn. "Dad!"

"I'm sorry, old friend." He leaned forward, tears thick in his voice. His body shuddered under my hand. "You were faithful. Well done."

I dropped his arm and searched the shadow where he kneeled. Crikey. A dead man, lashed against the wall just as my father had been. Questions rippled through my mind, but fear beat them down. We had to get out. Now.

"Dad!" I grabbed him and with all my strength jerked him to his feet. He followed and this time did not turn back.

CHAPTER NINE

"Let's not go." Eliza gripped my arm after we walked out the front door to catch the bus for school.

I looked at her face. The blue under her eyes made a haunting contrast with her abnormally pale skin. Terrified. She was absolutely terrified.

Me too. But I wasn't going to let it out. "We have to have an education, Liza. You know that better than anyone. What will we do as high school dropouts?"

"I don't think it matters anymore." She trembled. "Your dad—they almost killed him. He may still die. Please, Braxton. I don't want to go."

I tried not to think about my father. About the angry red rings around his neck and arms. About the broken skin on his skull, split from the force of multiple blows, or the sick yellow bruises that peppered his body.

Especially not about the dead man in the old factory.

Mother and I had managed to get him home before night fell. He'd done pretty well, all things considered, using us both for stability. By the time we'd gotten him back to the Knights' house and near a fire, his bare feet had been frostbitten. Another injury to look after, and nothing much to treat any of them with.

"Can't we get a doctor?" I'd asked.

"No one will see him." Mother continued nursing him, wrapping warm towels around his blue-tinged toes.

"How do you know?"

Father, only partially awake, rolled his head in my direction. "We're not sealed, son."

Standing outside the Knight's house with Eliza that cold winter morning, the memory of the chill in his voice penetrated my resolve, making my stomach quiver. Eliza was right —school wouldn't matter anymore. Not if we were going to remain among the Uncloaked. But bowing to them, hiding like scared little mice, was unthinkable.

I slid an arm around her shoulder and stepped down the sidewalk, pulling her with me toward the bus stop. "Come on. They won't do anything at school—it's too public."

She looked up at me, her weary eyes doubtful. Actually, not really doubtful. More like...like that look she gave when I said something she knew was ignorant, but she was too nice to tell me.

Am I ignorant? The police obviously knew about my father, and they'd covered it. His capture and beating were illegal, and they'd ignored it.

And what of the dead man? Murdered. He'd been *murdered*. Did the authorities know about that?

I slowed my pace, almost willing to give in and go home. I needed some answers anyway. Who was that man lying dead in my father's cell? What had he done? Father would be more awake today, and I could ask.

"Braxton?" Eliza tipped her head into my shoulder.

"Please, let's just stay home. Our parents, they'll understand. I know they will."

I glanced back to her house. The safe place. An image of a cockroach blipped through my mind, scurrying away from the light to hide in the shadows.

I am not a cockroach.

"It'll be okay." I squeezed her shoulder and trudged forward. "We'll stick together, and we will both be fine."

That image wouldn't budge from my head as we boarded the bus, a hard, cold air enveloping around us. Kids, both older and younger than Eliza and me, glared, which was becoming normal, but I decided the image of vermin was sent to strengthen my determination in the face of this hostility. *I am not a cockroach.* I repeated it over and over to myself while we rode through Glennbrooke. The nice houses of town—the ones not shut up with slabs of wood—sparkled with lights gleaming from their clean windows.

Farther down the route, the scene began to change as we traveled through the poverty section. The section where apparently Kipper Elliot had lived. Older, worn-down houses lacked the new shatterproof windows, and most of the openings left behind by broken glass panes had been covered over with sheets of shredded plastic or planks of saggy, misshapen cardboard. Smoke curled out of the chimneys, blanketing the dreary area with a heavy gray cloud that felt more hopeless than warm. People lived there. Many, if the amount of laundry hanging on droopy lines, the size of dormant root vegetable garden plots, and the junk piled up in the yards were any indication. No one stirred in the area—people stayed in their little hovels. Hiding, most likely. From the cold, the helplessness. Maybe from the Party. Staying out of sight, like cockroaches.

I am not a cockroach.

But I felt like a cockroach—one who'd been stupid enough to stand in the daylight while the giants of death brushed by me on every side.

The day didn't get any better once we arrived at school. I felt that heavy cloud of doom that had seemed to be symbolic in the poverty area. In the halls, in the classrooms, sealed students glared. Confirmed citizens mocked Eliza and me, barely concealing their hatred behind the flimsy screen of their hands. Were they talking about our living situation? Perhaps they were plotting our removal, like the Elliots'. Or were they whispering about my father? Had they known about that? All of them, had they known he'd been kidnapped and beaten—and none of them said a word? What was this, some bizarre form of virtual reality where people responded like heartless avatars in their mechanized sphere?

Eliza stayed with me. I wouldn't let her out of my sight. Our schedules hadn't been identical, but it didn't seem to matter. Our names had been removed from the roll list. We signed in anyway, which might have been a mistake. We probably should have stayed concealed—maybe our families would have drifted from the noncompliant radar if we'd remained quiet in the shadows.

But that was not how I did things. Loud and proud and foolish, that was me. Faults for which I was often rebuked by my father.

"Can we go home through the woods?" Eliza whispered at the end of the day.

The last place I wanted to be was trapped on a bus with the enemy. I nodded, slinging my pack over my shoulder. We left the building and crossed the school yard, and tension began to ease off my shoulders. I wouldn't make Eliza go tomorrow—in fact, if I had anything to say about it, she'd be staying home until this whole crazy situation blew over. She might miss the rest of the year, but it'd be better for her to fall behind a year than to endure this until the end of spring term.

I organized the arguments in my head, knowing I'd have to lay them out to her when I announced that I would continue to go. I wasn't as smart as Eliza—catching up for her would be a cinch. For me, it'd be next to impossible. And as far as taking the abuse, I could handle it. I'd been a preacher's kid since birth, and catching criticism was part of the gig. I'd be fine. But mostly—and I doubted I'd tell Eliza this, because it would require an explanation—because I wasn't a cockroach.

Lost in my conviction, I didn't hear the running behind us until a group overtook our path. Suddenly we were in the middle of a tight circle of boys, all dressed in the green jackets of the Jackals, and many of them seniors from our school, a couple of them conspicuously older and who should have moved on in life. Eliza went rigid at my side, and I wrapped a hand around her arm and stepped in front of her.

"Still protecting the little church girl, eh, PK?" Hulk's voice curled the hairs on the back of my neck. I turned my head to find him and then stepped around Eliza to fill the space between him and her.

"You can't protect her forever." He leaned to one side and sneered at her. "Not as an Uncloaked. Just look at your father, boy. Big man, he is, and a guy who had influence. Did anyone care when he disappeared?"

I swallowed. Hulk bellowed a hair-raising laugh. "Stupid boy. Do you think you could have taken him if we hadn't wanted you to?"

I shivered, clutching Eliza's arm.

Hulk stepped closer. "That's right, PK. We were watching. Saw the whole thing. Thought you were pretty brave, didn't you? We had a good laugh, watching you and your mother drag his pathetic body over the snow."

The cockroach scurried back to the darkness in my mind. *I am not a cockroach.* I lifted my chin. "Why did you let him go?"

Hulk smirked. "So you would know." He laughed again. "Tell all of the Uncloaked—and the Cloaked. Tell them what we're capable of. Tell them we are serious." He leaned close enough that I could see the black of his chaw stuck in between his yellow teeth. "Tell them what happens to the noncompliant."

A tremble started in my chest. I forced it to stop before it reached my chin. "If I tell everyone what you did, they'll know what you really are—a monster who will imprison us with fear. Do you really think the people will continue to support the Party then?"

His snort blew snot from his nose, which landed on my arm. I recoiled with disgust. Hulk traced my backward step, invading my space. "Idiot. Do you really think a lion full grown still needs its mother's milk?" His eyes narrowed, his deadly stare spearing my logic through the heart. "The people will comply. For love or fear, they will bow. One way or another, by force or by choice, PK, you will too."

Crossing his arms, Hulk leaned to the side again, casting his vicious glare on Eliza. "I hope you always protect her." All mocking vanished when he leveled me flat with a look of stone-cold intimidation. "There's only one way you can." He tipped his head to expose his marked neck and then stroked the tattooed seal. "Defiance will only end in misery."

Hulk stepped back, and the circle around us broke. The Jackals marched back across the school yard like a small brigade of a hellion army. Gooseflesh marked my skin, and I pulled in a quivering breath.

Eliza leaned into my back, and I could feel her tremble. I turned and pulled her close. Her body shook violently, but when she spoke, her voice came clear with the force of conviction. "Don't do it, Braxton." She pulled away and landed her pleading eyes on mine. "Don't ever bow to them. Not for any reason."

————

Healing my father became my mother's full-time job, which was fine because she'd lost her real one. Because we were Uncloaked. This reality finally sunk in. Mother was the most pleasant, competent person I knew. Her gentle ways mirrored Eliza's, and her intelligence matched my father's. The accounting firm wouldn't have fired her for any other reason.

For that first week, Mother not having a paying job became a relief. Evan Knight owned his own business—a pharmacy—so he still had work. Jayla, Eliza's mother, often worked with him. That left Mother, me, and Eliza to take care of my busted-up dad. Eliza knew quite a bit about what Father needed to recover. Her accelerated classes and her dad's occupation helped. But actually caring for Father? He was too big for her to do it alone, and I was too incompetent to be much help. Without Mother, Father would be in trouble.

"Eliza." Mother beckoned from the corner of the living-space-turned-recovery-room. "Patrick's head isn't healing right. Come tell me what you think."

"Did my dad look at it?" Eliza asked, moving to comply.

"He did. Last night." Mother slid back to allow Eliza access.

"It's fine, Anya." Father nudged her hand away. "You'll worry them."

"The gash is oozing today." Mother looked my father in the eye, pausing to silently communicate her concern, and then turned to Eliza. "What do you think your father would say?"

Eliza drew a breath. I thought she'd tremble or duck from my mother's gaze in the shy way she did when one of the kids on the bus would talk to her. She didn't. She looked Mother straight on and then stepped forward to examine my father.

I moved closer to watch Eliza's reaction. Mother brushed stray hair from the area behind my father's ear to give Eliza clear visual access. Alarm flickered in Eliza's eyes as she glanced to me for an instant before examining his cut more closely. "We should have stitched it."

"Your father didn't think so—too far past the injury."

Lifting two fingers, Eliza touched the area of their concern. Father grunted before he could stifle the sound of his pain.

"It's hot. Very hot."

Mother caught Eliza's eyes, and they held a meaningful look—one of near panic smothered by determination. "It's infected," Mother said, her voice low.

Eliza nodded. "I'll go to Dad's shop."

"No you won't." I moved closer. Visions of Hulk stalking Eliza's small frame jutted my shoulders straight. "You're not going to town."

She looked to me, her eyebrows quirked. "You're not my big brother, Braxton. I can handle myself."

"No you can't, not with Hulk." I glared at her, expecting that she'd drop her stare and comply. "He terrifies you, and you know it."

"Braxton." Father shifted as though he thought he could sit

up. He didn't make it more than an inch off the pillow. "Does everything have to be an argument with you?"

"Are you serious?" I fired back, letting my loose tongue roll. "You've been beaten almost to death by a bunch of armed hellion kids. The government turned a blind eye to your abduction, and you still want Eliza to go out there? She's been picked on by this brute long before this nightmare began. Do you really think he's going to lay off her because you need something for your boo-boo?"

"I want you to stop arguing with everything." Father glared through a painful squint.

My jaw went rigid, and I held his look. "I—"

"Braxton." Eliza stepped beside me, her fingers brushing my arm. Her voice dropped to a feather-soft whisper. "Just come with me, okay?"

Now she took on her shy, meek personality. I glanced down at her, and her brown eyes implored me to let it go. This was the girl to whom I could deny nothing. Was she playing that?

"Fine." My voice snagged somewhere between my throat and mouth. Maybe because Father incited boiling anger from me even when he was sparring with death. Maybe because melting under Eliza's gaze was kindling something way deeper inside of me than I was prepared for.

Emotions at war—and stuff I couldn't deal with. I let Eliza tug me out the back door. "Why are you doing this?" I hissed as we stomped through her backyard. "He'll survive until tomorrow."

"You need out of the house." She opened the gate that led to the creek.

"That's not why." I shot her a *don't you lie to me* look. "You were going, whether I came or not."

"Infections are bad. Blood poisoning can be deadly, and if you wait too long, oral medication can't fix it."

"How are you going to get him medication anyway, Liza?" I pulled her elbow, and she came to a stop. "Your dad's a pharmacist, and it's illegal to hand out drugs without a doctor's prescription. If anyone found out, he'll lose his license. Then what?"

Resolution emboldened her eyes again. "Daddy won't let your father die, which is what will happen if we don't treat this. Sometimes the right course of action puts us on a dangerous path—but it's still the right way to go."

I groaned, rubbing a hand over my face. "Not you too." I eyed her, my shoulders drooping. "Why'd you go all preacher on me? Don't you think I've had enough of that for my whole life?"

"I don't know." She lifted her chin. "You never listen to your dad, and whether he's behind a pulpit or dying on a couch, you've always gotta spar with him."

"Crikey, Liza. What are you doing to me?"

The fire melted from her face, leaving a soft glow of compassion. "I'm sorry, Braxton. I know sometimes he's... unavailable, and it's not fair. But he's your dad. He almost died, and he's not out of danger yet. What will you do if you lose him?"

"He's too stubborn to die." I looked away—her sincerity plunged into things I didn't want to face.

"His stubbornness may be exactly what brings his death." Eliza's voice dropped into that deep, reverent tone that sounded almost prophetic. "Are you prepared for that? Do you really want to face his death while you're still angry with him?"

Psychology 101. I hated psychology. I hated being probed

and messed with and challenged in areas where I didn't really have defenses. Besides, I had every right to be angry. He was everyone else's hero and my biggest disappointment. People said he'd drop anything for anyone at any time. They didn't understand I was the one he'd usually drop—and yeah, it was for just about anyone, and it was all the time.

"Enough." I hated the harsh growl of my voice. I didn't talk to Eliza like that. It was reserved for the man who provoked it.

But she was provoking it.

Eliza held her tender gaze for one more breath and then dropped it to her hands, which she twisted together in front of her coat. "Okay, Braxton." Her voice cracked.

I'd made her want to cry. My stomach lurched and then twisted, making me feel like what little was in there at that moment was going to come out. "I'm sorry, Liza." I reached for her shoulder and squeezed. "I didn't mean to snap at you."

"I know." She lifted her face, conflict written in her expression. "But...this isn't going to go away. You need to—"

"Don't bring it up again." I gripped her by the other arm. I wanted to shake her, to vent the anger I had stored up. No, I wanted to haul her in close, to siphon the comfort of her unwavering loyalty and unparalleled goodness.

I couldn't do either, so I released her. "Just, don't go there, okay? My father doesn't need to be a deal between you and me."

There was that look again, the one that told me I'd just said something impossible. But she nodded without a word, and we continued to follow the creek toward town.

CHAPTER TEN

"I'll need your help." Father turned his attention to me. Well enough after three weeks and a round of illegal antibiotics, now he had it in his head to go to the church. His reference books were in his office, and he'd decided they were unsafe on his cherrywood bookshelves.

I glanced out the back window from my seat at the dining table. Really, I didn't have an excuse. I couldn't go to school—they'd denied me access only a week after the Jackals had threatened Eliza and me. She'd known it was coming, but I wouldn't listen. Somehow, even as I accepted this reality for what it was, these slips into deeper un-American dictatorial living still came as a surprise.

How was all of this happening? Two years ago people would have been fined, or jailed, or stripped of their kids for not sending them to school. Now I wasn't allowed to go? Because I didn't get myself branded? Where all the American people in this? The ones who would fight for justice and freedom and equality?

They were sealed, that was where. Living as if life hadn't

changed and ignoring those who refused to go against their consciences. No, not ignoring. Persecuting.

"Braxton, did you hear me?" Father's commanding voice shattered the empowering effect of my silent rant. I wasn't on the side of the Party. But I wasn't sure I wanted to be on my father's side either. Because he was demanding—he assumed he could switch to a tone of authority and that would be enough to force his expectations. On me.

I lifted my eyes, settling them on him with a silent challenge. "I heard you." *Go ahead, old man. Demand my compliance. See how that works out.*

He held me in a wordless deadlock. A flicker of recognition passed through his eyes—something that didn't make sense. Suddenly his expression softened. "So"—his tone dropped to something more...friendly—"will you help your beat-up old man? I don't think I can carry everything back by myself, especially with a couple of broken ribs."

We were chatting? Like we were buddies? I worked my jaw, afraid that the part of me that longed for this since I was nine would latch on to it. And afraid that the other part of me that harbored every disappointment, every puncture of rejection, would refuse it.

"I'll come too." Eliza, who sat between us on my left, interceded before I could decide which side I wanted to win.

"No. You won't." I glanced down at her, hoping she could read me. I didn't want her between my father and me. I didn't want her to see who I was with my father anymore—it disappointed her, and I couldn't stand that. And I didn't want her to always play the referee between us, like my mother so often did. Eliza shouldn't have to, and it made my chest feel like it was being crushed by a LiteRail car when she did.

I shifted my attention back to my father. "We can handle it, right?"

Again he measured me. I hated that he assumed he knew what I was thinking. He didn't. He knew the vagrant off the street who came to him for whatever he came to him for better than he knew me.

"Right." He nodded, his gaze bouncing between Eliza and me.

My jaw locked as I scowled. Wipe that knowing look of your face. You don't understand anything. Not one thing.

Eliza maybe would have been proud of the way I held my words inside. Except, she'd be horrified that I thought them. How did someone as perfect as her end up friends with someone so ugly?

Shame curdled in my gut.

I swallowed, staring at my plate of not much breakfast. Small pile of scrambled eggs, half a slice of homemade bread, toasted. Two slices of canned peaches—stores from Jayla Knight's fall canning ritual. I should have been grateful—I was grateful. Without the Knights, we'd be dead on the street. Life shouldn't be uncomfortable for them because of us.

"We can go right after we eat, if that's what you want." I looked at Father without raising my head.

"That'll be good." He nodded.

Silence descended around the table, and I started on my eggs.

"Thank you for the meal, Jayla." Father set his fork on top of his cleaned plate. "We'll never be able to thank you and Evan for all you do."

I think his voice wavered a tiny bit. With a surreptitious glance, I checked his face. Humbled. Totally and completely humbled. For the first time in the months since we'd lived at the Knights', it occurred to me how humiliating this whole situation must be for my father.

But it didn't have to be this way. The seething voice in my head snuffed out the flickering flame of compassion. He was just stubborn. We were all paying because he's so stubborn.

A narrow thread of smoke curled where that small warmth had sputtered.

Father rose like an elderly man in need of multiple joint replacements. Clearing his plate, he stopped behind Mother. "Your bread gets better and better, Anya."

Mother glanced to him, her smile weak. "Practice makes perfect." She forced a brighter look. "Eliza said she'd help me today, so perhaps we can have rolls for supper tonight and bread for breakfast tomorrow."

He nodded. "Son?"

I pushed away the urge to spit out an annoyed response. Something like, The church will still be there in thirty minutes. Let me enjoy the little bit of food I have. "One minute."

He nodded and limped away.

Mother and Jayla both left, and Evan had long since gone to work. Hannah was off doing whatever she did—probably lurking somewhere nearby, as she often did. The room seemed to exhale with only Eliza and I left at the abandoned table.

"Will you be okay?" Eliza asked as she scraped the last bit of her eggs.

"Fine." I stopped eating to settle a look on her. "Why wouldn't I be?"

She tipped her face up to me, and after a moment of serious inspection, a small, sweet smile curled her mouth. "I could almost hear you wrestle with yourself."

Heat spread up my neck. "That so?"

94

She breathed a little laugh. "Yes. That's so. And the good guy won." Her grin faded a tiny bit, and her eyes softened.

I could love this girl.

Her hand caught mine and squeezed, and then she gathered her dishes and left.

Could she ever love me?

———

The crisp smell of spring drifted on the light wind as Father and I neared the church building. Eliza and I made this walk all the time, but with Father, it felt like the distance had expanded.

"Do you miss school?" Father asked.

"No, not really." I hated that we couldn't go though. Hated thinking about a future that looked about as promising as a green-tinged thunderhead in early May. But he didn't need to know all that—probably wouldn't care.

"How is Eliza taking it?"

Eliza was an off-limits topic. He probed when he was looking for something to unpack, something to examine and dissect, like a passage in the Bible that he could preach about later. My life—and my heart—weren't going on that list. Especially when what I found in my heart was scary.

Fear of the Party and of the future.

Anger with him. Unrelenting, boiling anger.

And something fierce and overpowering for Eliza.

He wasn't going to mess with any of that. Not ever. "You see her every day. How do you think?"

He moved his head, glancing sideways toward me as we approached the double doors. "Evan said she was pretty upset about being removed from the Career Track."

"Hardly matters now," I mumbled.

Again, he took a quick survey of my face. "She did the right thing, not checking the box."

The furnace inside of me flared. "Can we not talk about checking boxes?" I set a hard stare on him.

"Sometimes the hard path is the right one, son."

What the blazes? Could he not hear me, not understand that I didn't want to go there? "Crikey. You two sound like an echo."

"Who?"

Great. Way to open the door for further communication. Hadn't I learned yet that we couldn't do that? My father and I —we were never intended to talk. It didn't end well.

"Nothing. Forget it. Eliza did what she had to do, and she's convinced it was right, so you can save your sermon for Sunday."

Could be why our conversations never worked out nicely.

He stopped, but when I glanced at him, his smoldering eyes were not set on me. I followed his stare to the door of the church. Taped to the middle of the full-length glass panel was an orange notice.

Disbelief made me dizzy. Eviction? Of a whole church? What country was this?

My father moved forward, and I numbly walked by his side.

Due to noncompliance according to the Citizen Account-ability Act, and by order of the US DRA, this facility and all of its contents have been seized until further notice. This property is now in the possession of the US government. Trespassers will be handled by the PRP and will fall under discipline as seen fit by the empowered officials of the Party.

"What's the DRA?" The question tumbled out of my mouth as many others lined up behind it.

"The Department of Religious Affairs."

"That's a thing?"

His eyes darted to me. "Yes. It was established after Kasen signed the Religious Emancipation Act."

I stared at the door. "What does it do?"

Father turned to me, heat sizzling in his eyes. "This," he barked, tossing his hand toward the building. "It removes churches. It takes away our right to gather, to worship."

I scowled. That wasn't possible. There had to be more to it —something he wasn't telling me. "What does it mean, noncompliant? What didn't you comply with?"

He stopped pacing right in front of me and took a ready-for-battle stance. "You assume that I could have stopped this. You assume that if I played their game, everything would be fine."

"Well, is it true?"

He glared.

I crossed my arms. "What did they want you to do?"

"Give a roster. Names, not just numbers. How much every family gives. How often they attend." His face set hard, and I knew he'd die before he did any such thing. "It was all spelled out in a notice. I was to check a box stating that we would fall under the jurisdiction of the DRA, and as a token of compliance, I was to supply all that information."

"Check a box?" Fury took possession of my mouth. My fists doubled at my side, and I moved forward into his space. "This again? Check the dang box! Why are you so stubborn? It wasn't enough for us to lose our home, our dignity? Check a stupid, meaningless box, and everything would have been fine!"

He didn't flinch. "Don't you understand what that would mean? I swear undivided allegiance to the United States and hold unswervingly to the ideals of the Progressive Reform Party. No authority, on earth or in heaven, is above the power of the newly established order. Moreover, any claim of higher authority is punishable as treason. I can't agree with that, Braxton. To do so would be to deny God, and I cannot do that."

"It's a piece of paper."

He shook his head. "It's a statement."

"It would have saved everything."

"No, it would have cost everything."

I exploded, shouting in his face. "We *have* lost everything!"

My heart thudded recklessly while he stared. His mouth drew thin, and his eyes turned sad. "Whoever would deny me before men, I will deny before the Father." The verse lifted from his mouth in a hollowed whisper.

I hated when he ended a debate with a verse. It was like he'd stamped his victory with the approval of God, silently saying, *So there, foolish, biblically illiterate boy.*

"Well, at least I know your sacrifice doesn't end with your family," I spat, my ears still ringing with the force of God's Word.

"What does that mean?"

A derisive laugh vibrated from my chest. "You put us on the altar long before the Party took over."

Confusion tugged on his eyebrows. "Nothing's more important to me than God, son. Not even your mother. I can't deny that. But I don't—"

I shook my head. "You know what? I don't think that's true. I don't think it was all about God. It was all about appearances. About being everyone's favorite spiritual leader. The guy they looked up to and could turn to for anything."

He stared at me. But nothing came forward for several breaths. His eyes pinched in a painful expression, and finally he licked his lips. "I don't understand. Service to God means serving people. Why are you so angry about that?"

I snapped my mouth shut.

"Braxton?"

"Forget it."

"No, son, I won't forget it." He leaned in closer. "You tell me, once and for all, what soured you when it came to me. Are you angry that I'm a pastor?"

Rage locked in every muscle of my body. "No," I seethed, my smoldering glare pinned on his. "No, I'm angry that because you're a pastor you can't be my dad."

If I'd been flinging darts at his face, that one hit between the eyes. He winced, and then his face drew down. His mouth moved, but nothing came out.

Take it back.

I couldn't. Or wouldn't. Swallowing, I stepped backward. "I told you to forget it."

CHAPTER ELEVEN

"We can meet here." Evan Knight leaned forward at the table. "We're down to twenty, maybe thirty on a good day. We can all squeeze in."

Father's face looked gray. Illness from the injuries or defeat from the latest political blow? Probably both. Mix me and my rebellious spirit in there, and...

I cleared my throat, kicking guilt out of my monologue. He'd been fishing for it anyway. *Don't ask a question if you don't want to know the answer.*

Did I really hate that my father was a pastor? As a kid, I hadn't minded. We used to do stuff together as a family back then—and not just the church stuff. We went to Annyon's and Jamis's football games. Visited the coast. Ate dinner. Father's work had been an integral part of that life, but it didn't rob him from us. From me.

But things were different here. Coming home—back to my father's roots—was supposed to have been a good thing for all of us. In college by then, Annyon was playing football at Father's alma mater, a university not far from where he'd grown up. Father taking a pulpit in Glennbrooke was supposed to have been a way we could stay together.

Guess he didn't figure he'd still be idolized twenty-some years past his glory days. Or maybe he thought he was talented enough to keep everything within its checks and balances. More likely, I just didn't figure onto the scales.

"That'll be a big commitment, Evan." Father's brows drew into a *V*. "For your whole family. You've already taken us in. Consider how it will affect your family to offer your home as a meeting site."

I growled in the back of my throat and then pushed away from the table. "Thanks, Ms. Knight."

Father's attention turned to me. "You didn't finish."

"I've had enough." I stood, grabbing a roll before I left, and turned toward the stairway.

Eliza found me five minutes later. She lowered herself across from me in the dormer window of the upstairs hall, pulling her feet in close as she settled against the opposite wall. She studied the frost painted across the glass pane and didn't look at me when she spoke.

"No father-son bonding today, huh?"

I pulled my knees up to my chest. "I don't think that's possible."

"What happened?"

An open question—not one laced with accusation. Her gentle tone invited me. It was nice to have someone on my side. "He wanted to know why I'm not his fan."

"That's what he asked?"

I pulled in a long breath and let it out slowly. "Not with those words, but yeah. That's what he wanted."

She sat straighter, her look expectant. "And..."

I looked to the floor below the window, studying the

runner rug that covered the length of hardwood in the hallway. I didn't want to tell her how snarky I'd been. Not that she hadn't seen it before, but...but I didn't want her to see it anymore. I didn't want her to think of me like that.

"And then we argued about it." I glanced back to her, silently begging her to leave it alone.

Her eyes settled on me, large and gooey brown and...beautiful. Her steady breath came and went, sending faint puffs of white in the space between us. Warmth spread through me when she placed a hand on my shin. "I wish you'd let them see the Braxton Luther I know."

She knew *this* Braxton Luther. The one with a loose cannon for a mouth and who used resentment as daily fuel. What did she see in me?

"You never let me ride alone on the bus," she began, as though she'd heard my thoughts. "No one will ever get to me when you're around—you've even taken a fist for me."

I swallowed. Guys didn't tear up. That was the story anyway.

"And no matter how crazy I make you, you never stay mad at me."

My skin warmed, conquering the chill of the air while I stared at her. Did she mean all those things? How did she mean them? Did she know that in this stop-my-heart moment, all I could think about was how alive I felt under her touch?

She sat back, pulling back her hand and the hypnotic way she looked at me. With one hard thud, my heart restarted and reality smacked me in the face. Eliza had meant all those things, but she'd said them in an effort to motivate me to patch up my relationship with my father. Not to start something new...deeper...with her.

"They love you, Braxton." Her face averted as she again turned to the window. "Please, please...won't you try?"

Anger and desire toyed with my head, my heart. How was it possible for two opposite emotions to occupy the same space at the same time?

I followed her gaze to the smattering of delicate ice covering the window. Beauty and danger coexisting on one pane.

"Braxton?"

I felt her gaze on me again, but I refused to meet it. It might melt my resolve.

"They've had their chance."

———

Twenty-three people squished into the Knights' living room Sunday morning. Though he moved slowly and then sat on a stool set up in front of the crowd, my father's voice carried easily over the group.

"Faithfulness is not easy. But it is commended by our heavenly Father." He sat up straighter. "Let us not focus on the injustice. Many who have gone before us suffered. James tells us not to consider our trials as something strange but to embrace them as a confirmation of our faith. Let us look to the faithful who have gone on ahead, and we will find strength in their resolve."

Father paused, and his lips twitched. "We will not need to look far for inspiration." His deep voice cracked like a thirteen-year-old boy's, and his head bowed forward. "Thank you, Jesus, for our brother, Nathaniel Harper. We know he was welcomed into your presence even as he was beaten out of this world. Give us the same courage that we may stand against evil even when it costs our very lives..."

His prayer drifted into a soft stillness, interrupted only by an occasional sniff. The math wasn't that hard to figure, and I imagined old Mr. Harper's body still lashed against the dark wall in the factory. My eyes burned. How had he died? Why had he died?

"Come, Lord Jesus," whispered a woman from the back.

"Yes, Lord." The reply rippled among the gathering.

My father cleared his throat. "Our Father, who is in heaven..."

Voices joined in from every part of the room. I whispered the familiar prayer. "Your will be done..."

God's will. How could any of this be God's will? Did He will Mr. Harper to be beaten? To be murdered? What about the Elliots? They'd been sent to Reformation Camp—a place we'd heard more about as the days came and went. People went there, wherever it was, and they did not come back.

Our eviction. Father's capture and beating. The persecution. Was this all part of God's will?

What about the peace Jesus promised? Joy—where was that? Safety? We, the Church, were supposed to be God's people. Why was He not taking care of them?

"For Yours is the power and the glory..."

Is this what your god can do? I pictured with acute clarity the hand, brutal and strong, gripping Kipper's neck as the boy mocked his faith. Hulk. It'd been Hulk, I was sure of it.

"Forever and ever. Amen."

Amen. So shall it be. Except it was not. *Where are you, God?*

Sniffling permeated the room as silence once again settled over the people.

"Make us faithful..." Father's broken voice interrupted the stillness.

Make me faithful... A tiny voice echoed the prayer in the back of my mind. I wasn't sure how much I meant it. I examined my hands, clenched in my lap. They began shaking. Fear settled inside of me.

What do you believe?

The question, though in my head, came from somewhere outside of myself. I didn't have an answer. I knew the correct answer, but I wasn't sure it was true for me.

Glancing to my left, I caught Eliza looking at me. Her fingers brushed my elbow. *You okay?* she mouthed.

I looked away and nodded. She'd be mortified if she knew what I'd been thinking. So I stopped. Thinking. And listening. Only the burning sensation of weight and fear remained, and I worked to ignore it.

The service ended with me staring straight ahead, settled in a numbness achieved by a great concentration on nothing. Without song or signal, the tiny congregation stood and quietly left through the Knights' back door. I hoped we would not meet again.

———

"Braxton." My mother's voice whooshed in my ear, the warmth of her breath hot against my neck. "Braxton, get up. Go with Evan. Now."

She shook my arm in the blackness of a moonless night. I tried to focus on her face, pushing sleep into the recesses of my brain. "Why?"

"Go." With strength that surprised me, she jerked me upright.

The pile of covers I'd huddled beneath tumbled down to my lap. Freezing air hit my exposed skin like a blast of icy water. I shivered.

"What's happening?"

Mother didn't respond. I pulled my football sweatshirt over my head as I set my feet on the floor. No sooner had I stood, than my coat had been pushed into my chest. "Stay out of sight."

A crash of glass jolted me out of the fuzzy consciousness between sleep and awake. "Mom..."

"Now!" She pushed me into the hall, where a pair of hands clutched my arm.

I jerked away.

"It's me." Evan's deep voice calmed me. "Come."

"Upstairs!" A shout drifted from the floor beneath my feet.

Evan tugged my arm again, and I followed him into the room across the hall. Colder air pushed against my cheeks, and I slipped my arms into my coat. They trembled. Every part of me trembled.

"Evan, what's—"

"No time."

Boots pounded against the wooden risers down the hall. Evan pushed my head through the window, and I crawled onto the asphalt shingles covering their back patio roof.

"Crawl to the tree and stay out of sight."

A light flickered from under the doorway leading to the hall. Evan slid the window shut and moved back to his bed. The doorway flew open, and yellow light flooded the room. I flattened myself against the siding of the second story, careful to keep every inch of my body in the shadows.

"You!" barked a man inside. "Where is the Luther boy?"

"His room is across the hall." Evan spoke evenly.

Two more footsteps, and then the sound of a door crashing against the wall. My heart pounded with reckless ferocity. What was going on?

"He isn't here," called the same voice. His boots smacked against the floor again. "Where is your son?" His angry call had been aimed down the stairway. Silence answered his demand. Footsteps came back to Evan and Jayla's room. "You have a daughter, right?"

"Yes." Evan's voice dropped.

"Where is she?"

"In her room."

More footfalls. Oh, dear God, not Eliza. What was Evan doing? I scrambled back to the window. As I raised my hand to tap the pane, something pinged me in the back of my head. I whipped my neck around, my hands clinging to the house. Darkness.

"She's not here either," barked the rough voice from her bedroom.

I slunk back into the shadows, still searching the inky night. She was out there. She had to be.

"Where's your daughter?"

"She was in bed, last I saw." Evan's voice trembled.

"Do they often sneak out together, this preacher's boy and your girl?" Cruel laughter taunted Evan. "Under your own roof, no less."

My stomach turned as my jaw trembled. I could picture Eliza, her face growing pale and her eyes widening with pain. *Please, God, don't let her hear.*

"I've never caught them, if they have." Evan's voice continued to waver.

"Is it true you hosted a meeting here today?" The badger's snarky voice came nearer.

Evan remained silent.

"What was the nature of this meeting?"

Nothing. My rib cage hurt as my heart pounded against it. The air seemed colder, the night darker with each agonizing breath.

Boots stomped away, back toward the hall. "Burn it," the man yelled. "Take the preacher and his wife. Burn the rest."

Terror seized every muscle in my body. I scrambled across the roof toward the oak tree whose limbs spread over the Knights' backyard.

"Eliza!" I hissed into the blackness.

Something small and round struck my cheek. I looked toward the direction from which it came. A twig rustled in the tree. Stretching my arms, I reached for the thick branch above my head until the rough bark scratched against my palms. With strength I didn't know I had, I pulled myself up, swinging my feet until they wrapped around the limb, and then righted myself in the branch.

"My parents!" Eliza's panicked whisper reached my ears from two feet away.

I looked back to the house, through the window Evan had shoved me out of. Light from the hallway allowed enough vision to see a shadowed figure towering over two other forms. Zip-tying them to the corner post of the Knights' bed.

"Where's Hannah?" I whispered.

"Here." Her tiny frightened voice drifted from below me.

"Braxton, my parents!" Hysteria filtered into Eliza tone. "They're going to burn them."

I gripped her hand. "We'll get them out."

Commotion rustled from inside the house, down the stairs. "Move!" a harsh voice commanded.

My parents. What would they do to them?

———

Flames licked the upstairs hallway like tongues of evil laughing with malicious glee. Eliza whimpered in the darkness beside me, but I couldn't do anything until the sound of an engine cleared from the street out front. Chances were high that smoke would get to her parents before we did, but I couldn't risk being caught. Not with Eliza and her sister sitting in the tree right next to the house.

When the van's rumbling trailed away, I dropped from my perch to the roof. "Find something to break the window."

"They're pressure treated." Eliza landed beside me. "They won't break."

I pushed through the air until my hand found her arm. She shook violently beneath my palm. "I'll get them, Liza." I gripped her elbow and turned her toward me. Enough light filtered from the hall and through the window that I could make out the shadowy features of her face. "Get Hannah across the creek. I'll get your parents."

She gripped my coat in a fist. "Braxton—"

Whatever she was going to say, I couldn't handle it. Mission mode took over, and that unfamiliar courage filled my chest like it had at the factory. "Go. Now."

I didn't wait for her to move. Careful to keep my footing, I shuffled back to the window. Gripping the eaves of the dormer, I kicked against the panes. They shuddered but didn't crack. I took one more blow at it. The window remained solid. Eliza had been right, and I was wasting time.

With skittering steps, I made my way down the slope of the roof. At the edge, I dropped to my backside and then flipped onto my stomach. Ten feet of dead air separated the gutter from the ground, but being a long string bean would come in handy. For once. Pushing to the edge as far as I could without free-falling, I gripped the gutter. Without allowing time for more thought, I surged away from the roof, flinging my body into the air until my arms caught the slack. Momentum pushed me into a forward swing, and I waited until the motion switched, carrying me backward, and then I let go.

Four feet and a half a second later, I hit earth. The impact punched into my socked feet and rippled shock all the way up to my shoulders, but I stood straight, ignoring the jolt of pain. Picturing the lay of the house and yard in my head, I ran around to the front door. It hung open, allowing smoke to slip out into the night and a view of the flames crackling inside.

The street held in quiet observance. No sirens. No lights on in the neighbors' houses. Not one shout into the night to see if everything was all right. Just silence. Malicious, ugly silence.

I didn't stop to brood over it. Somehow I had to beat the flames up the stairs—which was unlikely since I'd seen them from the second-story window—cut Evan and Jayla free, and get them out of the burning house. Not a promising task. I didn't think about that either.

As if working off of muscle memory from some unknown practice in an alternative life, I stormed through the fire and up the scorched steps. My heavy coat protected me from burns, although the heat tinged my face with fierce vengeance.

Evan was sputtering when I reached him. Jayla had already passed out. Still on adrenaline autopilot, I ripped my pocket knife out of my coat pocket and started on Evan's hands. Two cuts and his hands were free. He spun to face his wife while I worked on her ties until they popped loose. Without communicating anything, I went for the window while he gathered her in his arms. Once it opened wide enough, I crawled out and turned to grip Jayla under her shoulders and dragged her onto the rooftop. Evan followed and dropped to his knees beside her. His mouth covered hers in the dim light from the house, and I heard him puff air into her body.

God, please let her live. For Eliza. Please don't let Eliza's mom die.

I couldn't even pray for my own parents. I knew, for them, it was too late. Part of me wondered why I prayed at all.

CHAPTER TWELVE

If I claimed Jayla's survival was a miracle, that would mean crediting God with kindness. I wasn't ready to do that. But she sputtered to life, somehow managing enough strength to get off the roof, and we set off for the creek. Evan propped her up and pretty much dragged her along by his side. I wasn't sure what to do, so I searched for Eliza and Hannah.

Darkness ruled the trees past the creek, the moonless sky a heavy cloak of black over the earth. We stopped at the frozen water's edge, and I glanced back to the Knights' house. The flames had overtaken the upstairs windows, and still no sign of help from any direction. It would burn to the ground. By the time the blaze finished, there would be nothing but ash where the stage of their lives had stood. No one would do a thing about it.

Desperately wicked...

Molten anger lodged in my gut. How could God allow such evil?

A series of hollow clicks stole my attention from the woods across the creek. Two low clicks, followed by one slightly higher. I licked my lips and answered by making the same sounds with my tongue against the roof of my mouth.

Click, click...click.

The black night air held for a moment, and then the call echoed back.

We'd made it up when we were ten. I had climbed our oak tree by the water on lazy summer mornings and waited for her to come out the back door to feed her dog. The first time I'd tried to get her attention by clicking, Eliza had frozen in the grass, cocked her head to one side, and waited. I had sniggered, which gave me away as she swiveled her face toward my place in the branches. I couldn't help it.

Our clicking call had become our secret code, though we didn't use it much anymore. Who knew we'd need it for real someday?

Click, click...click.

I moved in the direction of her call. After ten steps, I stopped. *Click, click...click.* Holding my breath, I waited for her response.

Click, click...click.

Eliza guided us fifty yards deeper into the forest. We nearly tripped on the log she and Hannah had huddled behind. I dropped to the frozen earth beside her.

"My parents..."

"We're here," Evan said. "Braxton got us both out."

Eliza's hand fumbled to my chest in the dark. She slid it to my shoulder and squeezed. I felt her tremble by my side, and though her father hunkered mere feet away, I wrapped both arms around her.

Muffled sniffling came from the form by her side. Hannah. Holding Eliza with one arm, I stretched the other across the inky space until I felt her hair. Another hand brushed mine. Evan's.

"What now?" Hannah's whisper cracked.

I swallowed. What indeed?

"It's only a couple of hours before dawn." Evan shifted, and Hannah moved as well. Probably to his lap. "We can go deeper in when there's some light."

Eliza trembled again. I tightened my hold. "Mrs. Knight," I whispered, "are you okay?"

"Yes." Her raspy voice didn't sound okay. Guess she figured she didn't have a choice though.

Silence enveloped us, and I leaned against the log. I refused to let Eliza go. Didn't matter what her father thought—if he knew at all.

My eyes stung from smoke and cold air. I tipped my head back against the freezing bark and shut them. Images of my mother and father swam against my eyelids. Scenes from the past, of us being together and happy. Dressed in matching T-shirts, they smiled and waved their hands in the air, cheering after Annyon had made his tenth sack of his senior season. Sober and teary, they held hands as we boarded the LiteRail car that would bring us to Glennbrooke for good. That was the last memory I had of them together. Really together. Oh, they were still married, still committed to their vows, but their lives...

Our lives. Something happened to our lives.

I pinched my eyelids tighter, ignoring the moisture that seeped against my lashes, and banished those images. Besides, they were together now. *Until death...*

Had that vow been fulfilled tonight? Where had the Jackals taken them? Were they, in fact, together? Would I ever know what had been done?

My jaw quivered. I tried to stop the questions from surfacing, but they were like cork in a scummy pond. They surfaced and floated until they were saturated with misery, and then they sunk into the deep places that could not be probed, left to spoil and fester in my soul.

A shudder rippled over my body. Eliza slipped both arms around me and squeezed. "I'm sorry, Braxton."

Her soft words barely drifted to my ears, and the emotion in her voice turned the vise tighter in my chest. I bit my bottom lip until the emotion passed.

I would not cry for them.

———

Light finally brimmed into the stark forest. Two hours had felt like days while we shivered through the darkest part of the night. We stood slowly, our bodies kinked and stiff from cold and fear.

"I know a spot." Evan turned to us, bending backward as he spoke to loosen his rigid back muscles. "Near the old barn, Liza. Do you remember?"

She peered up at her father and then nodded. "The cellar?"

"Yes." He nodded. "Down the slope from the barn but above the pond."

I glanced to Jayla, who still lay on the ground next to the log, her breath coming and going in a rough wheeze. "How far?"

"A mile in." Evan followed my stare to Jayla. "Eliza knows the way."

I turned back to him. "Where are you going?"

"Jayla needs medicine. We have to clear her lungs."

"Where do you plan on getting it?"

Evan's brown eyes settled on mine, communicating some kind of passing of responsibility. "I have a key to the pharmacy, hidden in town. I can get in."

"Daddy—" Hannah's choked cry was cut off by Eliza's hand.

Eliza looked terrified, but her jaw clutched in resolve. "I'll get us there. Braxton can help Mom."

I stepped forward, between Eliza and her father. "They burned down your house." I scowled at Evan. "You can't go to town. Right now, they think you're dead. You're better off that way."

"Jayla needs—"

"I'll get it." I punctured the air with each word, leaving no room for argument. "They know I'm still out here. If they see me, it won't give you away."

Eliza tugged on my arm. "They're looking for you."

"They were after my father." I looked over my shoulder, down to her, refusing to allow her pleading eyes to melt my resolve. Eliza needed her mom and dad. What they had together was special—and now they were all in danger because of us. Because of my father.

"They got who they wanted," I said. The plan was settled for me, and I wouldn't be persuaded. Besides, I was not a cockroach. I wasn't going to scamper out into the woods only to watch Eliza's mom die while we waited for Evan to *not* come back.

Eliza's eyes shifted from me to her father. She silently implored him. For me. She was begging him to not let this happen. The frozen pit in my gut began to melt a little bit.

"He's right," Evan whispered, denying his daughter her wordless request.

Her lips quivered. "How will he find us?"

Evan scanned the forest, his forehead furrowing deep. His gaze settled on me, softening to pity.

I drew my shoulders back. I didn't want pity. It made me weak.

"I'll manage. I'll stay out of sight." I didn't look at Eliza. Couldn't. She was the one person who could undo me. This was all there was to be done, and I would do it. Resolve hardening my jaw, I focused only on Evan. "Tell me what to get, where it is. You have to be specific."

He glanced to Eliza, and the compassion in his expression increased. I ignored it. "We need inhalers. At least five. Look for the ones labeled AreoHepN." He described the lay of the pharmacy, where I would find what he wanted. "The key," he said next, "is under the planter next to the back door. It's buried in the bottom. You'll have to crack the base with a rock, but try not to break the whole thing. Try to leave it so that no one can tell that it's been broken—that you've been there."

I nodded. Without turning to Eliza, I strode back toward the creek. I had no idea how I'd find the old dairy barn or the cellar where they would be hiding, but those details didn't matter at the moment. All I knew was that I had to fix the mess my father had left us in.

The town hadn't come alive yet. Shop owners slipped into their places of business, but other than that, the early morning had not yet been disturbed. My pulse throbbed in my veins as I snuck through the back alleyways. I clung to the shadows created by the brick buildings on Main Street. Evan's pharmacy was located at the north end of town, on a corner across from the town park, which made me more cautious as I got closer.

I hunkered behind the last building before the pharmacy, careful to check every direction for people. Or black vans. Only stillness met my inspection, so I darted the final twenty yards to the back door. A round planter, eighteen inches in diameter and full of frost-tipped, crispy remains of summer flowers, sat in the river rock on the left side of the steel entry. I grunted as I tipped it on its side, careful to hold the dead plants in place.

Glancing left and then right, I checked the area again for people. Movement by the building next door made my heart kick into my throat. My limbs tingled, and I froze, staring at the spot where I'd seen something brown dart into the shadows. I stopped breathing and demanded that my hands stop shaking.

The form reemerged. Small but bold. It came toward me. My chest hardened like granite as it neared.

"Eliza!"

She dropped down beside me.

"What are you doing?" My whole body shook. Not trembled. Shook.

"You don't know what you're looking for, and you don't know how to get back." She picked up a rock the size of a baseball from several that had been lined up against the sidewalk.

I ripped it from her hands. "You shouldn't be here," I growled, and then tapped the base of the planter. A crack fingered its way across the bottom. With a little more force, I knocked the weak point again. A porcelain triangle fell to the ground. I glanced back to Eliza. "Get out of here before someone sees you."

Her eyes narrowed, and she didn't flinch. "No."

My jaw clenched as I glared at her. "You know, you're infuriating when you do that."

She cocked her head, and a trace of sass lit those angry eyes. She stared at me for a breath and then began to dig in the hole we'd punched out of the planter's base. "That sounds like your problem." She pulled her hands out of the black dirt, producing the key, and then set her defiant stare back on me. "Not mine."

Crikey. Where'd she dig up that kind of gumption? If I hadn't been so dang mad at her, I'd have been proud.

I snatched the key from her fingers, ignoring the little tinge of admiration that threatened to tip my lips. "Of all the dumb things you could do." I flashed the electronic key over the sensor on the door. It buzzed for half a second and then beeped. I pushed on the handle, and it gave readily.

Eliza elbowed her way in front of me, her little back stiff and straight. "I'm not dumb. You don't always have to be so stubborn."

I followed her to the third aisle of shelves. "I'm not stubborn."

She snorted. "Yeah. You're not tall either." She grabbed a box from the middle shelf. "Get a bag from under the counter."

Whoa. Eliza Knight met...well, me, actually. Huh. I followed her directions, not entirely believing the whole scene or sure why I was letting it continue. Spotting the pile of sacks under the checkout counter, I marched to the front of the pharmacy and jerked out a handful. I had taken a step toward the back, when something in the park beyond the front window caught my attention.

I couldn't move. Breathe. Think.

There was a wide grassy spot where children would play chase and the older kids would toss a football. The middle of that open space was now occupied. A slab of steel, about ten feet long and four feet wide, consumed all attention. It was flat and tilted a little bit. On top of it, another slab hovered, separated by a gap created by a form. A human form.

My father.

"Braxton, what—" Eliza's irritated voice cut off. She gasped, the rush of air drifting from the spot right behind me.

I couldn't tear my eyes away from the horrific sight beyond the window. My father, a human sandwich, in the middle of the town park. A pair of Jackals stopped beside him to laugh. Spat in his face. One doubled his fist and landed a blow next to his eye before they continued on their way.

My stomach lurched. Heat poured over me, and my ears rang. I dropped whatever it was I had in my hand and scrambled toward the front door.

"Braxton, no!" Eliza's hand snagged me before I got past the counter. "You can't go out there."

I couldn't see straight. The world blipped in some kind of wild, unintelligible series of light and sounds. I pushed away the hand that gripped my arm and leapt over the counter.

My vision narrowed, focused solely on my father. Sounds blurred together, a collage of some kind of wicked laughter and shouts. None of it made sense. Didn't matter.

"Dad..." Out of breath, and my pulse throbbing, I dropped beside my father.

The contraption holding him wasn't just bondage. It was torture. Six large screw jacks, three on either side, kept the slabs pressed together. The tops of those jacks rotated slowly, tightening down the pressure ever more with each meticulous turn. The tilt of the bottom table held him at a downward slope so that the blood in his body drained toward his head.

My father's red eyes turned to me. They bulged, matching

the blue veins puffing under his forehead. His labored breath wheezed in and out, and with every inhale, the table constricted even more.

A modern-day stoning. Advanced technology designed for medieval torture.

Desperately wicked...

"Dad..." I choked on the taste of vomit.

"Brax...ton," he rasped, and then tried to pull in another breath. The pressure on his body wouldn't allow his lungs to fill. "...can't be here..." Tears leaked from the corner of his eye.

My throat closed over. Every muscle in my body quivered.

"Son..."

I opened my mouth, but my voice wouldn't work. What was happening? Where were the people—all of those who had followed my father when he'd pastored their church? All of the ones he'd helped during their greatest crises? He'd led a congregation for years, sacrificed his time and his family for their spiritual good. And now...nothing?

That was what Eliza had warned about, wasn't it? Christians...who refused to stand.

Apathy is the illness of the overprivileged...

My father hadn't been addressing the country at large. He'd been speaking to us. Me.

"You're strong." My father's real voice interrupted the memory of his sermon, spoken so many months before. His whisper seemed stronger than it should, backed by the power of conviction.

My head moved side to side. "I'm not," I cracked. "Not like Annyon and Jamis. Not like you."

His eyes got soft as he looked at me for a long moment. "You"—he drew another short breath—"are most like me."

A shadow passed over him, and then a hand jerked my shoulder back. I lost my balance and landed on my hip.

"Finally made it, eh, PK?" Hulk towered over me. His green jacket barely fit over his muscled shoulders.

A surge of anger zipped through my core. I didn't bow to bullies. Jumping to my feet, I jammed my chin up. "What are you doing to my dad?"

"He's being pressed." Hulk's icy stare held mine and then slithered to my father. "The old fool will not comply. His influence is too great to ignore, so he will either publicly swear allegiance or publicly die." He leaned over, staring my father in the eye. "Your choice, old man. This could all be over with one little word. Will you yield?"

My gaze bounced from my father to Hulk and then back again. *Yield!*

"No." The strength in that one syllable belied the agony of his crushing suffocation.

"Dad!" My harsh whisper barely escaped my lips.

Hulk looked over his shoulder and then laughed. "Don't worry, PK. We have a place for orphans."

I drew back. "Where's my mom?"

Hulk's snort sounded like an overstuffed sow's. "Her train left hours ago." With a long smirk, he held my stare. "You're on your own now, PK. Hope you make some better choices than your father. Especially for that little church girl. I hear Reformation Camp isn't very nice."

Eliza. She was with me. Where did she go? I concentrated on *not* looking for her so that I wouldn't give her presence away. *God, please keep her out of sight.*

Hulk stepped beside me and smacked a hand to the back of my head. "It doesn't have to be this way, Braxton." His arm curled around my neck and squeezed. He leaned in close, his voice snaking into my ear. "Think it through carefully. Remember, we see everything. You really can't hide."

He pushed me away, and I fell to my knees. The crowd that had gathered to hear our exchange loosened and then broke away. Jeers filtered through the air, but all I really could hear, could comprehend, was the wheezing, shallow breaths my father struggled for. A blue tinge circled his mouth, growing more distinct as his skin faded into a papery pale hue. His eyes continued to bulge unnaturally from their sockets.

"Brax—" One more unsatisfying breath. "Do not bend."

I stared at him, waiting for his next labored attempt for air. It didn't come. His look went vacant, and every part of his frame became still.

Deathly still.

Do not bend...

My lips quivered. I bit them, denying the hot tears in my eyes an escape. Check a box—keep your house. Check another box—keep your job. Say a few meaningless words—keep your life.

Do not bend? I wouldn't.

I stood, taking one last hard look at my father. *I am nothing like him.*

CHAPTER THIRTEEN

THE NIGHT AIR SLICED AGAINST MY SKIN LIKE AN ICY blade. I couldn't bring myself to go into the cellar. Hunkered in that dark cave was a family. United. Used to be that was why I liked hanging around the Knights. Now it pierced the secret places of my heart, a place much deeper than the frigid chill could touch.

The vivid stars gleamed in a cloudless sky above my head, mocking my angry wounds. Distant beauty. Beckoning the imagination and yet forever unreachable. I shut my eyes, wanting to block out their twinkling laughter. My father's lifeless eyes replaced the nighttime canvas.

They would forever haunt me. I'd never be able to shake the vision of my father, murdered in the middle of town. For what? For exercising what had once been considered an American value—to hold fast to his faith?

Noncompliance. That was what the Jackals had said. That was why he'd been executed.

Why couldn't he just work with them? Nothing of this nightmare would have played out this way if he'd just been a little bit open minded. He didn't really have to deny God, not inside his heart. Just cooperate with the powers that be. How could that be so wrong?

"Was it worth it?" My angry growl cut into the silence as I stared back into the heavens.

The stars winked a jeering answer, making my stomach burn. *Orphan*, they seemed to tease. *Your father left you orphaned.*

We have a place for orphans. Hulk's tobacco-laced breath clung to me, as if he still breathed in my face. I rubbed my neck.

"Hey." Eliza jarred the agonizing silence with her wispy voice. Her hand brushed my shoulder, her feathery touch the only warm bit of reality in my surreal trance.

I couldn't look at her. Facing the expanse of black that dropped down into a pond that had secretly existed all these years, I drew in a quivering breath.

She had met me by the creek after I had wandered through the town, having abandoned my covert operation. People had snorted, glared. Some had cast looks of unvoiced sympathy my way. None of it sunk any deeper than a mild awareness. My father's death cocooned me, wouldn't allow anything to penetrate past the empty knowledge that I was alone...an orphan. Forsaken by a father who hadn't been that interested in me in the first place for a God who hadn't seemed to care. Anger had nearly filled the shell of my existence, until Eliza's hand slipped into mine.

We had walked side by side, hand in hand deeper into the forest. She didn't speak. Didn't ask me if I was okay—because unlike me, Eliza didn't ask stupid questions.

Jayla had tried to console me with a motherly hug, but she was too grieved and appalled to do much of anything else.

Evan had broken down too when Eliza whispered what happened. I separated myself after that. Their anguish wasn't like mine. It wasn't tangled with rage and resentment.

Just before sunset, Eliza had brought me a chipped mug filled with something clear and steamy. Probably hot water. I didn't know though. Didn't touch it. She squeezed my shoulder and left me to my misery. That had been hours ago.

Now her fingers curled over my shoulder in the darkness, and then the warmth of her body filled the space by my side. She looped her arm through mine and then leaned her face against my bicep. Her touch became the only thing holding me to sanity, and I reached with my free hand to cover hers.

Silence filled the woods. Her wordless compassion became a blanket over me, and it began thawing the frozen rage lodged in my heart. I wasn't sure that was a good thing—I didn't want to feel. Not like this. But she kept still beside me, and I couldn't will away her tender effect.

Words suddenly trickled from my lips. Words I didn't think about, didn't fully understand. "I have no one."

Her fingers wove into mine. "You have us."

I turned to her, studying the outline of her face. "Just you." A lump suddenly took occupation in my throat. "You're all I've ever had."

"Oh, Braxton, that's not true." Her breathy sigh ruffled the night, and then she squeezed my hand. "It's okay to admit that you loved him."

My heart of stone cracked just a little. I didn't like it.

Sitting up straighter, I looked back out into the blackness. Scenes from the past eight years clicked through my mind. Over time, my father became buried under his responsibilities at church, and I became...unimportant. He went from coaching my sixth-grade football team to...completely preoccupied. Unavailable for anything that involved me.

"Do you remember last year, the game where I actually got to play? I kicked it to the five-yard line, and then it just died." My voice seemed lifeless, like the empty feeling that had settled in my core.

"Yeah. It was your best punt."

I turned my face back to Eliza. "Do you know where he was?"

Her silence answered my question.

I snorted a laugh. "Sorting out some dumb squabble between ministry leaders at church."

Emotion caught in my throat. Pain, crushing, unbelievably heavy pain suddenly filled every corner of my soul and made me tremble. Eliza turned enough to reach for my other shoulder and pulled me into an embrace. Another shudder rippled over me, and then I clutched her close, pulling her onto my lap. My arms shook, and my lips quivered. I buried my face into the hair that fell around her neck. Though my hold was fierce, Eliza didn't object. Instead, her arms circled my neck, and with one hand, she held my head.

I didn't know how long we sat curled together in a lump of terror and ache. She didn't break away from me until I loosened my hold. Liza was like that. She never put rules over people. She seemed to instinctively know the needs of others and understood that love met those needs even at the price of propriety.

There wasn't a single person on the planet like her.

Hulk's menacing voice snuck back into my hearing. *Hope you make some better choices than your father. Especially for that little church girl.*

Resolve hardened in my chest as her arms untangled from

around my neck. Eliza Knight was a precious gem, one who should be guarded at all costs. I had to protect her—and I wouldn't fail the way my father had failed my mother and me.

My mind notched into a decision. There really was only one way to keep her safe.

———

I followed Eliza back into the cellar. She had been shivering, and I'd told her to go inside. She refused with that one-word stand that she'd become so good at.

"You shouldn't be alone," she'd added after a strained silence.

I needed to be alone because I needed to formulate a plan —something that I rarely did and was not very good at. But I couldn't just leave in the morning without an explanation. Evan would ask questions, Jayla would worry, and Eliza...

God, help her to understand.

She wasn't going to. Eliza had been begging me with her silence not to do what I knew I must do long before my father's death. Telling her, warning her, would do nothing but cause an argument. And that wouldn't change my mind, no matter how right she always was.

Muffled breathing floated from the corner of the musty shelter. I hunkered down against the cold earthen wall opposite of the sound. Eliza settled beside me and then blew out the candle she'd left lit before she had come outside. She leaned against me as darkness shrouded us once again. Total, utter darkness.

Cockroach. I clenched my jaw. We were hiding in a hole of darkness like vermin. Eliza Knight was not a pest to be exterminated. She shouldn't have to live like this.

No one should have to live like this.

Where had my America gone? Two years before my greatest disappointment had been not attaining the rank in my class that would allow me access to the best education. But I had been warm and safe, not hungry and hiding for my life. Suffering had been defined as staying at church for a late board meeting. Dreams had been right in front of me—possible. I just needed to study harder, get better.

Now we were holed up underground, living in a nightmare.

Had my father seen this coming? If he had, why didn't he comply? If he knew the cost of his willful resistance, why hadn't he negotiated a better deal? Death would be his legacy. What kind of a heritage was that?

An infectious one. One that, like Ebola, would not cease its path until each one of us had been ravaged. But I knew the vaccination, and I'd take it before Death tapped his cold finger on Eliza's beautiful heart.

But she wouldn't understand all of that. And wouldn't accept it.

My muscles grew stiff and cold in the damp air while I waited for Eliza to go limp at my side. The steady breathing across the room continued; her parents and sister slept through my darkest night. My eyelids began to sink with a heavy demand for sleep, but I pushed my shoulders straight and drew in a long breath.

A plan. That was what I needed to work on.

The forest would stay dark for quite a while, even after sunrise. That would be to my advantage, because I didn't want to be seen. Not by the Knights, but especially not by anyone who was *not* one of the Knights. I couldn't imagine anyone knowing of their well-hid shelter, and I didn't want to be the one to breach their secret. I would sneak away as soon as Eliza slept, and then wait at the forest's lip, by the creek, until the day was fully underway.

Surely the Party headquarters was the place to start. From there, they would tell me what to do.

———

An icy drizzle met me when I emerged from our hollow. The heavy gray cloak of clouds shrouded the early-morning sun's weak attempt to warm the earth. I shivered in my coat as I carefully closed the hatch door to the cellar. It hadn't been exactly warm down there, but at least it'd been dry.

Ignoring the ache in my backside and the tingles running up and down my legs, I forced myself to turn and walk. If I had stood there contemplating either the miserable dripping from the sky or the shelter that I'd just abandoned, I might have lost my resolve.

Maybe that wouldn't have been a bad thing. I stopped and braced a hand against a tree while I looked over the frozen pond that rested in the slight depression of land. Who could find us here?

Do not bend.

Father would be ashamed if he knew what I was about to do. Livid, actually. He died believing he had stood firm—and he had. That was what he'd been talking about when he told me not to bend. But in standing firm, he'd allowed evil to overpower him. That was what he couldn't see and what I couldn't understand. How could God intend for us to live like...cockroaches?

My stomach rolled with queasy revolt. I looked back to the slanted entry to the cellar.

Eliza had slept against me. Made me feel like I was her safe place, her comfort. I wanted to be those things. Leaving her required me to shift her away from my shoulder, to have her curl up on the ground by herself.

A chill poured over me, and I touched the spot on my arm that she had warmed.

With a stern command, I forced my gaze away from the cellar, from Eliza, and back to the frozen water. I recalled the horrible things I'd seen over the past six months. Kipper and his family, publicly humiliated, beaten, and then packed away. My father, kidnapped at gunpoint, beaten, and left to die with a corpse rotting across the room. The Knights' house, torched. My mother...just gone. Forever, and I'd never know for sure what happened to her.

My father's execution.

The Jackals knew I was alive. Eliza too. They wouldn't let us slip into hiding. Because I was Patrick Luther's son, and she the resolute church girl. With the Party, it was a *comply or die* demand, and we had become a threat.

Because of my father's unyielding determination. Eliza had become a target because of him.

That iron feeling of intent returned, quelling the nausea in my stomach. She would not suffer as my parents had. I wouldn't allow it, and I had the power to prevent it. This was the only course of action.

I pushed away from the tree and began picking my way through the maze of trunks and roots and shrubs that made up the forest. Following the light etching of gray on the horizon, I continued eastward. The wet and dreary morning held quiet under the oppressive sky, the earth too, it seemed, afraid to arouse itself before the Party. But life went on, and so must I. With a plan.

What had taken Eliza forty minutes to weave through yesterday took me close to two hours on my own. Nothing in the woods seemed familiar, and I was sure that I'd never find my way back. A good thing. The Knights were well hidden.

I pictured Eliza alone on that earthen floor and then pushed the image away. Someday she would understand.

The creek suddenly breached the thick tangle of trees, and I paused, standing on the threshold of a new boldness. There would be no turning back now. Scanning the backside of the neighborhood that had been our home, I chewed on my bottom lip. My sight landed on a black blotch along the trail of suburban houses. Charred remains of the Knights' house. I shuddered, but my determination feasted on the sight.

This is why.

I pushed my shoulders back and stepped toward the creek.

"Where are you going?"

My heart stalled as Evan's voice drew me back into the trees. I hesitated to look at him. He knew.

"Braxton, what are you doing?" He approached me close enough to squeeze my shoulder and yet remain under the cover of the trees.

I stared at the pile of rubble and ashes where their house had stood. It wasn't hard to picture the blaze devouring all of their earthly possessions. I could see Evan and Jayla, still bound to their bedposts. And I imagined Eliza, caught in the flames.

I moved away from Evan's reach. "I'm doing what must be done."

"Don't." He stepped closer to the creek, farther from the shelter of the woods. "You can't do this. Come home with—"

"I don't have a home," I growled, "and neither do you."

He stood motionless. I turned and focused, dead set on his

eyes. "Your ideals, my father's ideals, they will kill us. It doesn't have to be that way."

Weariness and grief mingled in his eyes. "Your father was a good man, Braxton. I'm sorry—"

I slashed the air between us. "Don't be sorry! Be smart. For Hannah and Jayla. For Eliza."

He stared at me, that knowing look that my father used to wear smeared on his face. "This will devastate her," he whispered.

Arrow dead center. Because I knew he was right. I dropped my defiant glare. "It's the only way."

"Only way for what, son?"

Air filled my lungs, and I stood straight. "I'm not your son. I'm not anyone's son." I broached a step closer. "And since you refuse to ensure Eliza's safety, I will. I'm not going to let them snatch her life away."

He didn't smolder the way my father would when I challenged his authority. He didn't shrink either. "Do you think that taking their seal will change what they do?"

Logic and arguments, not my best playing field. I functioned on anger and reaction. I couldn't let him persuade me though. "I think that it will change what they do to *me*. And to Eliza."

Evan stared at me as his steady breath painted puffs of white into the air. Calm never left his countenance. "When I was a small boy, I would visit my grandparents at their dairy farm." He turned back to the forest, to the abandoned farm where his family was hiding. "I remember a day when my grandfather had to load some unproductive cows to send them to slaughter. The animals didn't resist. They followed willingly.

"I asked my grandfather why. He was sad, because that

part of the job did pain him, but it had to be done. He said, 'Evan, they follow the hand that has fed them. They do not know they're being led to their death.'"

Evan turned his head and focused his gaze on me. His eyes, which resembled Eliza's in color, begged me to yield.

I swallowed, and my stomach quivered again. His look was too intense, so I turned away. Scanning the block of houses again, I focused on the Knights' home. He couldn't be right. Everyone else still had a home. They ate food, real food. Their kids were safe. They weren't cattle being led to the slaughterhouse. They were living the American Dream.

Evan was wrong.

"I'm not a cockroach." The words tumbled breathlessly from my mouth. "I won't hide like a cockroach. The next election will end all of this chaos, and then life will go back to the way it was." I turned back to Evan. "If we cooperate, we'll get through this with our lives and our dignity. It's only to survive."

"What good is it for a man to gain the whole world and yet lose his soul?"

Evan's quotation snapped my calm. "The preacher is dead," I snapped. "I would not recommend you take his place. He died in agony because he was so stubborn."

I didn't wait for him to respond. With steps marked by determination, I left the shelter of the woods. Even when I passed the skeleton of his house, I didn't look back.

From now on, my future lay in my hands. I would submit to the ruling power so that I could protect Eliza's future.

CHAPTER FOURTEEN

"You are incredibly stupid."

Hulk's voice stopped me cold. I'd made it to Main without anyone even glancing my way. If I could just make it to the Party headquarters, I could get this over with and move on with life. Maybe they'd let me stay in my old home, since I would be a verified citizen. Maybe I'd gain the equalization rations and be able to eat my first real meal in months. Maybe...if I'd made it without Hulk noticing me.

With measured steps, Hulk circled me from behind. His nearing presence rippled gooseflesh on my arms. Hate boiled in his eyes as he pinned me with a glare. "What are you doing, walking in my town? Did you not understand what we did to your father?"

I stared back at him. "I understood." I thrust my chin forward. "I am not my father."

One bushy eyebrow quirked up. "Really?" He crossed his muscled arms. "Then what are you doing here?"

My pulse throbbed in my ears. I drew one breath through

my nose and then released it slowly. "I've come to"—my hands trembled, and I shoved them into my coat pockets—"to pledge."

One corner of his mouth slid upward into his cheek. Hulk rocked back onto his heels and then threw his head back, and the air trembled with his evil laughter. He looked back to me with a smirk. "Wise up, did you?" Another snicker broke from his nose. "About time. The Party always wins, PK." He leaned in close again, and a menacing gleam lit his eyes. "Always."

I held his look. Hulk didn't need to know I wanted to puke. Our silence extended, allowing our stare-down to do the talking.

I'm not afraid of you. I didn't want to be, anyway.

Hulk's top lip curled. *You should be.*

Why? What can you do once I'm sealed?

Hulk took a military stance and broke our wordless confrontation. I wanted to believe I'd won that round, but Eliza's face swam in my mind. He'd leave her alone after I'd been inked, right? I would be trophy enough. Patrick Luther's son, pledged to the Progressive Party. They didn't need Eliza. She wouldn't be worth their effort. And they couldn't find her anyway.

Stay by the pond, Liza.

Maybe telepathy was a real thing. I hoped. If she would keep hidden, everything would be okay. I'd figure out how to keep them fed, how to keep them alive.

Just stay, Liza.

She never listened when I told her things like that.

"Come on, then, Preacher Boy." Hulk sank an iron grip on my shoulder. "If you're going to be sealed, I want to see it." He pushed me onward, toward headquarters.

My legs felt heavier the closer we got to headquarters.

Father's voice tickled in my ears—*Do not bend*. Tears, unwelcome and unhelpful, suddenly glazed my eyes. *I'm not, Dad. But Eliza...*

Very strange. It'd been years since I'd had a real conversation with my father. I'd given up trying somewhere around age thirteen. Tired of being brushed off or told that *now's not a good time. I have...* Fill in the blank. Meetings. A sermon to finish. A home to visit. A man to pray with. Ministry planning.

He was a one-man show at a church large enough to need at least three pastors. And I was the distraction he couldn't fit into his schedule.

But today as my blood throbbed through my veins right before I became the greatest disappointment in Luther history, I wished I could have a real conversation with him.

I don't know what else to do, Dad. I can't let them get her.

What would he say? I imagined all sorts of easy, slide-off-your-tongue answers. *You can't betray God, not even for Eliza Knight. He will take care of her.*

Would he say that?

I stopped walking, realizing we were in front of the heavy double doors of City Hall—Party HQ. Disturbing, but even more so was the new awareness that I didn't know my father. I knew the preacher, but I didn't know my dad. Now I never would.

My eyes shut, and his face, his dying, tortured face swam in my mind. I sucked in a long breath.

What should I do?

Hulk's hand crashed onto my shoulder and then squeezed. Hard. "Second thoughts, PK?"

My eyes flew open, and I shot him a look. His upper lip snarled.

Second thoughts? Couldn't happen. He'd kill me himself, right there on the street, and then who would protect Eliza?

I shoved his gorilla hand away. "Get off me." Squaring my shoulders to him, I set a dead-certain gaze on his menacing glare. "You can't touch me anymore, got that? I'm in—or am about to be—and I'll be protected under the Citizen Recharacterization Act."

"Oh-ho." He laughed. "Big man, are we? Filling your dad's shoes?"

As if that could be done.

"No." I dropped the word like it was a lead ball. Learned that one from Eliza.

Hulk opened the door and swept his hand to the side. "Let's go, big shot. No turning back now."

I held my place and his stare for two breaths and then stepped into the enemy's roost with make-believe confidence. No turning back. Because Eliza needed me here, whether she realized it or not.

———

A uniformed PRP official squared to me, his face severe and his voice solemn. "Hold up your right hand."

Who exactly was I swearing by? The Party rejected God, in any measure. Man was supreme above all things—we evolved that way, so that was the way it should be. History had been forged by our hands. Our future, too, would be forged by our hands. The supernatural was fiction. All that we saw and knew was all that there really was. Anything beyond that was fairy tales.

Who was closed minded?

I slipped my right hand into the air.

"Repeat the following." The officer stared at me without flinching. "I swear undivided allegiance to the United States and hold unswervingly to the ideals of the Progressive Reform Party."

I repeated the first sentence, forcing my voice not to quaver.

The man continued, still grave. "No authority, on earth or in heaven, is above the power of the newly established order."

I swallowed. *To do so would be to deny God...* My father's conviction swirled through my head. Clenching the fist I held down by my hip, I shoved his voice away. "No authority"...my hands trembled..."on earth or in heaven"...nausea rippled the lining of my stomach..."is above the power of the newly established order."

God, I don't mean it like that. Please don't let me puke.

"Will you uphold the Party and its authority with every breath of your life?"

Wasn't that a little...fanatical? "Yes, I will." Not really. I'll do what I must to keep Eliza safe.

"And do you understand that if you are found to be insincere in your pledge, you will be charged with treason?"

And punished by death. Murdered. That was what would happen. Cloaked, Uncloaked, it was all the same. Resistance, rebellion would not be tolerated. This was the new order of the United States of America. From freedom to bondage, happily voted in by the people.

Cattle led to the slaughter house. Evan had been right. And now I was branded—almost. But I could see things for what they were. I still wasn't on the side of the Party, but I needed Eliza to be safe.

"Do you understand?" His harsh voice demanded my attention.

I focused on his narrow expression. "Yes. I understand."

His gaze didn't falter. "Good. Turn to your right, go down the hall, and take the first door on your left. The inker will give you our seal."

Hulk palmed my shoulder before I took a step. "He should be directed to the Jackals as well, sir." He grinned some kind of sly *I've got you now* kind of grin. "He's an orphan, you know."

The man's slicked silver head bobbed. "That is the place for him then. We take care of our youth." He glanced between us and then addressed Hulk. "You can take care of that, Garrison. Get him set up and settled in. Uniform, dorm, the works. Make sure our new family member is comfortable."

I eyed him. "Family member?"

"Yes." A smile finally cracked his rigid mouth. "We take care of our loyal youth. No one should be without a family. Don't you agree?"

Did I have to answer that? I closed my mouth.

"Ah, I see." He tipped his head to one side. "You'll see, young Luther. This family will not disappoint you."

———

The laser stung, but the inking process didn't take long.

"You're official," the inker said. Her grin, though stretched wide on her glossed lips, didn't say *I'm so excited for you*. It said...I don't know what it said. Something grave or sad. "Almost no one has a reaction to the ink, but if it swells or you feel your throat closing over, get to a clinic. Only an inker can remove it—and that can only be done for medical reasons. Otherwise attempting to remove the seal is subject to criminal discipline." Her eyes held steadfast on me. "Treason."

Treason. My stomach rolled. Maybe I'd already committed treason. I pulled up Eliza's soft profile in my mind. This was for her. *For her, God, okay? Or are you even listening?*

Anger punctured my heart at the strangest moments. Like this one. Perhaps, though, my blood turned hot because of the subtle indictment of the spirit. Treason? Who betrayed whom anyway?

When things would get hard, my mother used to tell us to count our blessings. Leaving everything I knew to move to the Midwest: *Count your blessings, son. Glennbrooke is one of the prettiest places you've ever seen. We can be glad we're not going to a tribal bush somewhere in South America.* Not gaining the expected Luther physique: *Count your blessings, dear. You're growing tall. Some children don't grow at all, and then there are real problems.* Failing the Career Track test: *Count your blessings, Braxton. You still get to go to school. You can still try for a higher education.*

She'd always follow her well-meaning pep talks with her version of scripture. *Our Father clothes the lilies of the field and feeds the ravens in the sky. He will always take care of you too.*

This great protector and provider, the God she loved all her life, what had He done? Did He stop the brutal boys who kidnapped her in the blackest hour of night? Did He rescue her before they pushed her onto a Reformation Camp–bound train? How about now? Was He watching her while they did— the tightness in my stomach made it hard to breathe—whatever they do there?

"I'm not a traitor." I stared hard at the far wall as the words seethed from my lips.

A hand clamped onto my shoulder. "Better not be," Hulk

growled. "The worst of discipline is reserved for the double minded."

My legs trembled, and hot moisture suddenly filled my eyes. God had said that too, I was pretty sure. I was in trouble either way.

But I hadn't betrayed anyone who hadn't betrayed me first.

CHAPTER FIFTEEN

"Let's go then, PK." Hulk smacked the back of my shoulder like we were long-ago football buddies.

I sent him a scowl as we walked out the big double doors. "Braxton. It's Braxton. Think you can remember that?" I must have a death wish. Probably. But Eliza needed me—maybe I should check my tongue.

Hulk snorted. "Emboldened already." He gave my arm a fist bump and then turned to walk up the sidewalk. "See what kind of freedom you've found?"

Freedom? I just signed over my life to a party I hated because I was terrified for the one person left in the world who mattered to me. In what universe did fear equal freedom?

"Yeah, I'm liberated."

He stopped midstride and jerked me to a halt by one shoulder. "Watch it, Luther. That seal you just took? It means that you're one of us. Better take that seriously." He bent, pushing his face into my personal space, making sure he had my undivided attention. "Your father's death—that was kind compared to what we do to those who betray us." His stare burned into my eyes, and then he tapped my skull. "Let that sink in. Let it swim in that hard head good and long, because I know your soft spot. I know where to hit so it'll hurt the most. There are far worse things than death, boy."

My gut burned as Eliza's dark-brown eyes passed through my mind. Yeah, he knew. And what he could do...bile burned in my throat.

"Got it, PK?"

I clenched my teeth—didn't want him to see my jaw tremble—and returned his penetrating look. With my spine straight and after a long breath, I seethed a response. "It's Braxton. I'm not anybody's kid. Not the preacher's, not the Party's. I'm just Braxton. Got it, Hulk?"

His eyebrows pulled into a *V*, and his nostrils flared. I doubled my fists while preparing my mouth for impact, but Hulk suddenly cracked a grin. And then a laugh.

He crossed his arms and rocked back on his heels, still chuckling. "You'll do."

I'd do what? I didn't move, didn't break my glare pinned on his face.

He turned back to the direction we'd been walking and started off again. "Let's go then, Braxton. Your new home awaits."

Home...not likely. Home was a girl with sweet, chocolate-colored eyes and thick, wavy dark hair. Home was feeling her warmth against my arm. Home was wanting to be the guy she thought I was.

Home was not in the Jackals Den.

I followed him while emotions swirled like searing heat waves inside my chest. I wanted to go home. To beg for Eliza's forgiveness. My feet shifted into autopilot, and I let my mind drift back there. Surely by now Evan had told her.

Was she crying? Maybe she was staring at the pond, anger dark in her pretty eyes, disapproval engraved on her forehead.

Please, Eliza. Please understand.

A much worse vision pushed into my imagination. Terror clawed at my throat as I pictured her in town, following me, calling out. *Braxton, don't. Don't ever give in to them. Not for any reason.*

My heart raced, its rough pounding near explosive measures. *God, please don't let her come here.* I'd rather she stay in the woods hating me than to have her show up in town.

"You'll recognize our quarters." Hulk's voice snapped me back to reality.

I did a quick scan around us, checking for Eliza. She wasn't among the young men who peppered the parking lot we'd reached. I froze as realization smacked me, and it took a few breaths before I could raise my eyes from the lot on which we stood to the building I knew sat at the end of it.

A chill rippled over my whole body. I swallowed, forcing my gaze onto the brick-and-steel structure rising before me.

"Should be easy to settle in, eh?" Hulk blew out a laugh. "You've spent half your life here already."

My core trembled. The church. Now an ominous symbol of how much life in America had changed. Outside, it looked almost the same. Bleached stones, one stacked on top of the other, complemented by industrial-steel beams and teak wood, made the building look modern and not so much churchish. Except for the cross tower. I couldn't stop my inspection from traveling to that focal point.

The cross had been razed. Gone completely. At the top of the tower, where the two beams should have called to the masses of broken, needy people—people who longed for hope and for a life beyond the dismal reality of living—a fist clutching a sledgehammer rose out of the stone.

Shaking to the heavens. *By our hands.* Shouting to the people. *There is no God.*

Everything inside me quivered. Sweat dotted against my forehead, and my eyes burned. I tried to draw a breath, but it seemed the oxygen couldn't travel into my lungs. Panic surged through me, paralyzing me.

"It's a sight, isn't it?"

I didn't care who was talking. I wanted him to stop. My right fist clenched, and without understanding what I was doing, I found myself hurling into the air, straight toward Hulk.

A pair of large hands gripped my shoulders from behind. "Easy, Luther."

I knew that voice. My pulse pounded in my ears as I spun around. With a commanding stance and clad in the Jackals uniform, Jedidiah Stevens held me with a measured look. "Just take it easy." He glanced to Hulk, who hovered behind me. "I'll see to him, Lieutenant. Don't worry about it."

Drawing another breath, I fought for control. I couldn't protect Eliza if I died right there in the church parking lot ten minutes after I'd been sealed.

Hulk stepped around me and leaned back into my space. "Don't forget what I told you, Braxton. You know I won't." He scowled, his eyes holding a dark promise. "I'll be watching you."

"You have drills to oversee, young Garrison," Jedidiah intervened. "Best get to it."

Hulk's eyebrows quirked, and he sent a none-too-respectful glance toward Jedidiah.

Jedidiah held his place and returned the look with a hard stare. "Now."

After bouncing a glare from him to me, Hulk pivoted on the blacktop and stomped away. I watched him go until he reached the double glass doors. Doors on which only months ago I'd seen an orange eviction notice. Something hard and cold grew in my chest. I shifted my defiant stare onto Jedidiah Stevens.

He spoke just as my lips parted. "Keep your mouth shut for once, kid." His eyes drilled icicles into mine. "If your life matters, which it must a little bit because you're here, you'll learn how and when to shut up. Got it?"

I examined the frigid stone of his face. He could stop a grizzly in the middle of a full-on attack with that stare. It reminded me of someone else's... It reminded me of my father's. Except...not. My father's solid *I will not be moved* expression came from conviction. Hard-core, deep-set, worth-dying-for conviction.

Jed's did not. Fear frosted his stoic look.

Suddenly I felt like I was face to face with a mirror. I hated it.

———

"Tristan, you have a bunkmate," Jed barked across the lot.

I turned, and my vision collided with Tristan. The Elliot snipe. What had I done? Why was I there? I didn't want to have anything to do with any of these people.

Eliza. That's why.

Tristan neared us, looking as though he was marching. Across a church parking lot. Weird. Didn't anyone here understand how strange all of this was?

"Take Braxton to the haven and show him around," Jed said.

"Sir." Tristan tipped exactly one nod. I expected him to salute and actually found it off that he didn't. "Let's go, PK."

"Braxton," I clipped. "Braxton or Luther. You pick, but those are the only options."

Tristan laid a sideways glance on me and smirked. "How about Benedict?"

That was supposed to have some meaning, I was sure. I wasn't sure what though. Eliza would know... My chest hardened. Sometimes the right thing was the hard path. Protecting Eliza was the right thing. It had to be.

Tristan's snort-laugh snapped me back to reality. "No comeback, Luther?" He paused, waiting for his bait to work. If I knew what he was talking about, maybe... He snorted again. "That's a first."

Huh. My mouth had quite a reputation. I pressed my lips together and continued forward, trailing Tristan by a step. He glanced at me again, only this time the smirk was gone. Some kind of understanding passed through his eyes.

I looked away.

At the door, Tristan stopped. He looked to me, then to the glass panels of the entry, and back to me. "You ready?"

What exactly was he trying to prepare me for? I'd been in this building a million times. I should probably be showing him around. "Whatever."

He pulled in a long breath and then tugged on the black handle. Who knew Tristan was such a dramatic guy? I scowled as he stepped through the door in front of me, wishing he'd just point me to our bunk room and then leave me alone.

Same building. Not the same place. The air pressed heavy in my lungs. The walls, which had proclaimed various Bible verses cut out in vinyl the last time I'd stepped foot in this hall, now shouted Progressive propaganda. Posters, ordered from one end of the hall to the other, reminded every Jackal passing by the Reformer's creed: *I Am Power.* A man's bare muscle-ripped shoulders set the background for that statement.

We Are One. A dozen clenched fists gathered in a circle supported the claim.

By Our Hands. The fist and sledgehammer.

I trembled as a wave of gooseflesh surged down my neck, over my shoulders, and on my arms. Darkness seemed to drape over the natural light from the windows. Not a darkness seen, but felt. I pulled in a long breath, trying to calm my pounding heart, but the air quivered in my lungs.

Was this what it felt like to be without God?

Tristan stopped at one of the entries to the worship center. The bunk room now? Talk about communal living. People actually wanted to coexist that way?

"This is the Commons," he said. Again he paused, his hand resting on the door, as if he was waiting for me to prepare myself. "We hang here. Everyone hangs here." His eyebrows rose—a warning, I think—and then he pushed open the door.

Darkness, this time real, cloaked the vaulted room. The transom windows had been covered with thick black cloth so that nothing of daylight could touch the interior. I squinted as my eyes adjusted. Electric lights glowed over the stage up front, but not the kind that illuminate. The black-light kind. A haze hung over the room, making it difficult to identify the shadowy forms scattered across the expansive floor.

I inhaled, still trying to calm the clawing panic in my chest, and then wished I hadn't drawn such a deep breath. A pungent musk slithered through my nose and cast a thick film in my lungs. My head seemed to expand and fill with something light and confusing. I closed my eyes, and the room moved beneath me.

Tristan's hand gripped my shoulders. "Steady." He spoke low. "You'll get used to it."

I opened my eyes, and sparks dotted the murky space. I squeezed them shut again. "We hang here?"

"Yes." Again a warning—or a demand. Probably both.

"What do we do here?"

Silence pierced my murky conscience. I could imagine what happened here.

"Anything," Tristan whispered, a thread of shame hemming his voice. "Everything."

Shame? This guy turned in the Elliot family. Beat them and then sent them on a one-way train to God knows what. And yet whatever they did here made him ashamed?

My stomach rolled, and the wave of nausea about took my feet from under me. Tristan's hand caught my shoulder again, keeping me upright.

"We have to do what is necessary, Luther," he said as if he'd read my thoughts. "You know that. I know you know that, or you wouldn't be here."

What did Tristan know?

Fear twirled in my gut, wrapping me in a new barbed wire–like bondage I hadn't known existed. I was among the Cloaked now, and at least one of the Jackals knew it.

CHAPTER SIXTEEN

A BULLHORN BLASTED THE STALE AIR, AND WITHIN TWO breaths, the bunk room buzzed with motion. Feet thudded on the floor as Jackals pulled on pants, slipped into thermal liners, and tugged on boots. When did I sign up for military camp?

I planted my socked feet on the hard floor. "What are we doing?"

"Morning drills." Tristan ducked into his liner. "Get dressed."

"What happens if I sleep in?"

He shrugged. "Find out, why don't you?"

Better not. Not on my first day. I glanced around the dim room. Boys playing army. I wanted to laugh, right up until the wicked orange-and-yellow tongues of an arsonist's fire danced through my mind. Not funny. Hellion kids armed for terror. And now I was one of them.

Hulk's large face suddenly dropped in front of mine. "Move, Luther."

Why was this guy always popping into my face? Didn't he have anything better to do? I stared at him, an eyebrow cocked.

"Oh-ho," Hulk snarled. Still hadn't brushed his teeth. Never did—I was surprised he still had any. "New guy thinks he's something." His eyes narrowed. "We'll see."

He stood straight and settled his fists on his hips. "Since Luther here thinks he's up for it, we'll do five miles instead of three. After that, hand-to-hand drills. Get to it. Nobody falls behind."

Five miles? Please, let's not be running five miles.

Yeah, we ran five miles. I wanted an oxygen mask and a bed. And some breakfast. Did we get to eat in this crazy Jackals military school? I had a surreal, hover-over-the-situation moment as I followed the rest of the Jackals into a local gym on the other side of town. The whole military army game seemed oddly humorous in a sick, twisted sort of way. These people were serious. Deadly serious. And that made it funny.

I needed more sleep, and probably food. Nothing about this life was funny.

"Rolls are in the conference room," Hulk shouted over his shoulder. "You have five minutes to stuff your face before maneuver drills." He stopped and pivoted an about-face. The group split around him like water around a stick as they continued forward. His eyes roved over our faces until he picked out mine.

You're mine, he mouthed.

Oh good. I was wondering.

Fresh bagels and hot coffee waited on long tables in the conference room. Finally, something good out of this ridiculous club. I fisted two rolls in one hand and a full cup of black coffee in the other.

"Easy, Luther." Tristan stepped beside me. "You'll get sick."

Bagels made you sick? I glanced down to the food in my hand and then eyed Tristan.

"When's the last time you filled your stomach?" he asked.

Oh, we're rubbing that in now. I shrugged and then ripped a huge bite from one of my bagels.

"Okay. Whatever, Luther." Tristan shook his head. "I won't try to help you anymore." He walked away without a backward glance.

I watched his back and then looked at my breakfast again. Maybe I should go a little slower. It had been a while since I'd filled my stomach. After putting one bagel between my teeth, I stuffed the other into my coat pocket. Just in case Tristan was right.

Hulk meant five minutes, and apparently everybody else took him seriously. Still chewing, I followed the line into the gym and started removing my coat because everyone else was.

"Luther." Hulk's taunting voice carried over the group. "You and me."

The sea of Jackals parted, leaving me a pristine walkway to the mats. My mouth had landed me in fist fights before, but those never worked out well. I touched my nose, feeling the knot just above the bridge where Hulk had broken it last time. That had been one punch, and he hadn't had months of combat training to power-pack his drug-enhanced muscles.

I was as good as dead.

My feet carried me forward, though I didn't remember telling them to. All the drama of the past year, and I would end up dead at the hand of the same bully who had been picking on Eliza and me since we were twelve. Was that irony?

"What's going on in here?"

Hulk's attention ripped away from me, and I followed his look across the room. Jedidiah Stevens stood with his feet set in a solid stance and his arms crossed over his chest. "This doesn't look like class drills, Lieutenant."

Hulk pivoted and mirrored Jed's stance. "I'm calling Luther out."

"He just joined us."

"Never too soon to prove yourself."

Jed shook his head and scowled. "Not on his first day."

Hulk crossed his arms and then snorted. "Right. Like we don't all know your real reasons."

One of Jed's brows hiked into his forehead. "Best you get to work."

"Sure thing, *sir*." He flung a wimpy salute. "We'll all just ignore the fact that you're only out to protect the prize of the Den."

———

Sweat soaked the back of my thermal shirt, sticking to my skin. The jog back to the Den was pure torture. My legs screamed their indignant exhaustion. This was what all the Jackals hype was about? How could I sign out?

"Ten minutes to shower. Lunch is in the mess hall today, and then get to your classes. No exceptions."

I was pretty sure Hulk gloried in the fact that someone—someone irreconcilably insane—had given him full reign to rule the Den. Apparently the most muscle got the most control. Typical. So much for the equalizing promises of the Progressive Party. Like that would ever actually happen. What was that saying? I was sure I'd read it in my history app—one of the few lines I'd actually scanned and remembered. *Absolute power corrupts absolutely.* Something like that.

How about when power started out corrupt? Shivers ran down my arms. *You get us—that's what happens.*

I stripped my soaked shirt off my back and gathered the toiletries I'd been given yesterday. The others trickled out of the bunk room, destined for the showers. Tristan held back, waiting for me.

Trust was a luxury a group like this couldn't offer, but Tristan was the closest thing to a friend I was going to wring out of this situation. Surely he'd answer a few questions. I kicked my boots under my bunk and glanced at him over my shoulder. "What did Hulk mean, prize of the Den?"

"You're the gold-medal convert, Luther." Tristan tried to force a smile. "The pièce de résistance."

"Synonyms aren't helpful." I glared at him. "I need to know why."

"Seriously? Can't do elementary math?" He rolled his eyes and tossed his stinky clothes into a canvas bin waiting at the door. "The great Patrick Luther's son. A Jackal. You don't think that gets notice in the ranks?"

My eyebrows pulled in. No. I apparently couldn't do elementary math.

"Why do you think your family didn't get singled out and sent on the LiteRail with the others?" Tristan shook his head. "Why were you allowed to move in with the Knights, rather than being shipped out? Think, Braxton."

My father was that big of a deal? I mean, I knew he was in the Christian culture, but to the Party? Why would they care that much about a midwestern pastor? Like he was actually a threat or something.

"Look." Tristan turned back toward me, his dark skin threaded with power through his bare chest, another threat of intimidation in my new world. Was every guy in this Den ripped?

And I'm the prize? Someone's crazy.

"Your dad was the prize they were after. If they could gain his cooperation, most of the resistance would follow. After he made it clear he wouldn't, under any circumstances, comply, they made an example out of him. You weren't the only one terrified after his execution."

He stretched, pushing his palms up to the ceiling. Pretty sure so I could appreciate the fact that muscles defined every part of his torso. And I thought I felt like a string bean next to my father.

"Now you're a Jackal." He dropped his arms and then pulled one across his chest to stretch his shoulder. "Think there's a chance they're not going to parade that in front of anyone still insane enough to resist? If Patrick Luther's son is on the side of the Party, why would anyone else question it?"

My father was a pawn? A political move on a life-size chess board? Okay, maybe that made some sense. He was, after all, nearly idolized for more than twenty years. But me?

"They've got the wrong son," I mumbled, tossing my own dirty clothes into the bin.

"What?"

I darted a look at him and then dropped it to the floor. "I'm not their poster boy. If they wanted a standout Luther, they came after the wrong guy."

Tristan snorted. "Whatever. Why don't you go convince leadership of that theory?" He propped his hands on his hips. "No one around here even knows you have brothers. You're the guy—Luther's son. You were who they went after. Guess you took the bait."

Bait? Which bait? My father's murder? Protecting Eliza?

"Better watch your back too." Tristan stopped moving, showing off. "Hulk's not gonna have it, you know. They want you to move up the ranks, maybe even take his spot. How do you think that's gonna go over?"

All I wanted was a warm bed and a full stomach. And for Eliza to be safe. I'd definitely stepped into way more than I'd expected. "What if I don't want it?"

"Did you want any of this?"

The bonfire I'd attended so many months ago surged through my mind. I could see the wicked fire consuming the pages of the Bible, smell the drug-tainted smoke, hear the roar of rebellion. The sense of fear had only increased over time. No. I didn't want anything to do with the Party.

Treason lay on the tip of my tongue. I clamped my mouth shut and walked away.

CHAPTER SEVENTEEN

Bass rhythm vibrated the walls. I closed my eyes in our nearly abandoned bunk room. Twelve Jackals shared this space—what had been the classroom adjacent to my father's old office. That room now held the Den director. It didn't take more than one guess to know who held that position.

Jedidiah not only worked in my father's office but lived there too. Without his wife, which perked my musings. It also didn't escape my notice that his son hadn't wandered past my vision. I'd been sealed for a week—the kid ought to have surfaced in seven days' time.

I opened my eyes and stared at the platform above me. "What happened to Andre?"

Tristan rustled against the thin foam pad, and after a couple of breaths his face peered over the edge. "Don't ask too many questions."

My eyebrows rose. "That was only one question."

His mouth twitched to the side, and he fell back against his bed. "The Jackals redefine family."

"So?"

"So keeping the bond of blood in the mix might be dangerous."

Family was dangerous? The Stevens had been one of the first to hop headlong into the Progressive movement after the election. They did it as a family. Wouldn't that be a good thing for the Party?

I traced the fist and sledgehammer carved into the plywood above me. "Why?"

"That's three questions." Movement crackled above me again, and Tristan's feet dangled in front of my face. He grunted, and then he was on the floor, crouched in a landing position like Spider-Man. "Three too many. No more." His green eyes dark with warning, he raised his eyebrows as if to close the discussion and then stood. "You haven't been to the Commons since the first day."

Yeah, there was a reason for that. A strip club would have been rated PG in comparison. Nothing like a crowd of high, power-hungry, and emancipated almost adults who possessed zero conscience to redefine depravity. My face burned as I tried to wash the images from my mind.

"It's expected," Tristan said.

I opened my eyes, which I hadn't realized I'd shut, and looked at the wall behind him. I sat up and placed both of my boots firmly on the ground. Go to the Commons? No way. The nightmares had been vivid and sickening after that one experience, and I couldn't shake the vision of Eliza forced into... Bile filled my mouth.

"Braxton, Hulk's not going to let it slide much longer." He slid onto my bunk beside me. "You know he's already got his suspicions."

I hadn't figured Tristan out yet. With certainty, I knew he'd been behind Kipper Elliot's removal from known society.

He'd been all-in Jackal back then. But now? He was holding out and protecting me, and I couldn't calculate why. I eyed him, sitting there by my side.

"I'm going out tonight." I pushed off my mat and stepped toward the door.

"Where?"

My progress didn't stop as I stomped to the door. "Out."

Silence followed my back. I didn't turn to see if Tristan had too.

I reached the creek as the gray of evening gave way to the dark of night. A hint of smoke still swirled in the air, though the charred remains of the Knights' house had been scooped away by machinery and hauled somewhere else. Didn't matter. The blaze from that night still flared in vivid sizzling color inside my mind.

The ground squished under my boots, and I didn't risk wet pants by walking out on the soft ice. A running leap would put me on the other side, but that ran a little too close to risky in my estimation. I wasn't planning on seeing her tonight. Just wanted to be near.

With my back pressed against the cold, rough bark of our oak, I waited for the stars to wink through the budding skeleton above and banished thinking from the moment. I wouldn't listen to the echo of my father's last words. Wouldn't visualize Eliza's tears when inevitably her dad told her what I'd done. Wouldn't imagine—

Click, click...click.

I snapped to attention, squinting into the woods across the creek. Erie silence settled all around. After a glance to my left and then to my right, I licked my lips and returned the call.

Click, click...click.

A buzz started at the base of my head. I should go back.

Shouldn't let her near me. But I couldn't. Instead of spinning an about-face and heading back to the Den, I searched the darkness of the forest and listened for her response.

Click, click...click. Closer.

I checked to my left and right again, and then behind me. Nothing. My stomach turned, but with two rapid steps, I jumped across the creek.

Click, click...click. Slightly to my left and in front of me. I followed her signal. The cooler microclimate of the forest pricked against my face as the fading light dimmed. Stepping over a log, I scanned the branches, wondering if she'd hid above ground. Suddenly a hand slipped into mine, and I spun around. She pulled me behind an oak whose girth concealed her frame and wrapped me in her arms as soon as I was close enough.

"Liza," I breathed against her head. "You shouldn't be here." My arms locked around her shoulders even as I spoke.

She pressed her forehead into my shoulder, and her fists clutched the back of my coat. I inhaled the scent of her hair, earthy and smoky and yet still Eliza. My eyes slid shut, and the muscles in my arms squeezed tighter. She whimpered but still clung to me. Was I crushing her? Or had something happened? I wasn't sure what to think.

"What are you doing here?" I willed my arms to unlock, and gripping her shoulders, I stepped back to see her face. "You're not safe here, Liza."

Dirty trails cut down her cheeks, but she'd stopped the tears. I reached to trace the path near her nose, but she pulled away.

"I had to see for myself," she choked. "I told Daddy you wouldn't do it."

My chest tightened, and I froze. She reached for the collar

of my coat and pulled it away from my neck. She seemed to shrink as she stared at the seal, and she snatched her hand away as if she'd found something toxic.

Bottom lip trembling, she backed against the tree. "You did it." A tear slipped over her eyelid. "How could you, Braxton?"

A burn of anger lit in my stomach. "Don't go preacher on me, Liza. I did what was necessary to keep us safe."

"Safe?" She pushed her shoulders straight and thrust her chin up toward my face. "Are you safe now?"

Her eyes smoldered. My chin quivered. The Den wasn't safe. I was under constant watch, and what happened in the Commons made me want to curl up into a fetal position and cry. But I hadn't done this for me.

I took a step closer and glared down at her. "You are. I did this for you."

Eliza raised her hand, and it flew at my cheek, but she stopped it before her palm smacked my face. Her eyes widened, and she jerked her hand away, but in the next moment she shoved me with every bit of strength her small, starving frame could muster.

"Don't you dare!" A sob stole her voice, but she pushed me again. "I never asked you to sell your soul for me, Braxton Martin Luther. Don't you dare say that this was for me. This was what you wanted all along. What you wanted your father to do. What you thought all of us should have done."

Hot tears stung the corners of my eyes. Rejection from Eliza. The worst possible scenario. But I'd known it would happen. Didn't soften the blow.

"I didn't sell my soul, Eliza." I shouldn't argue with her. She always won, and sparring would make it worse. But walking away, having her hate me without understanding, that wasn't an option. "I got a tattoo. That's it. That's all this is."

"Oh." She crossed her arms. "How silly of me to be so dramatic. This isn't any big deal. The Party is nothing. Why would I think otherwise?" Her arms fell to her side, and she doubled her fists. "Wait. Maybe because they stole our lives. Burned our house down." She stepped close enough that her hot breath fanned against my neck. "Murdered your parents."

I grabbed her elbow and squeezed. She didn't fight me, didn't back away. Didn't drop her blazing stare. Her anger and disappointment bore deep into my heart, splintering it into pieces. My jaw trembled, and I bit my bottom lip. "Please, Eliza..." My hoarse voice cracked.

Suddenly she was tangled in my arms again. I didn't remember her moving or me pulling her close, but somehow we stood in the darkening forest, wrapped together. Crying.

"Don't hate me," I whispered near her ear. "You're all I have."

She didn't respond, but she didn't let go either.

Time became irrelevant. I hadn't wanted anything more than wanting to stay with Eliza, hidden in the forest and enveloped in her arms. Nothing more. Just her warmth seeping through my coat, the love I hoped she felt for me thawing my cold heart.

An owl screeched in the distance, and then something rustled behind the tree, toward the creek. Night had descended completely. What was I doing? Eliza shouldn't be anywhere near town or me.

"You need to go." I stepped back again, putting an arm's length between us. "You're not safe here."

She reached across the space I'd put between us and caught my hand. "Come back with me." Her thumb traced my knuckles. "Please, Braxton. They don't know where we are. They won't find us. You don't have to do this."

A breeze set the tree branches in motion, crackling above our heads. My senses returned full force, and I searched for movement in the forest. Every twitch and sputter in the darkness set the hair on my neck stiff. They would find us. Me. They'd been after me since the day they'd burned her house down. Now that I'd pledged, they weren't about to just let me walk away.

"Eliza." I gripped her shoulder. "I can't. You have to go. Don't come back." With one tiny step, I closed the space again and then tipped her chin up, as if she could see my face in the darkness. "I mean it, Liza. Don't come back."

She sniffed, and a tear dropped onto my fingers. I turned my hand, tracing the wet trail to her nose and then fanned my fingers across her cheek.

Leave. Now.

Dropping my hand, I stepped past the tree. My vision blurred, but it didn't matter. The darkness covered my tears, concealing my shattering heart. I continued to walk away.

I had to do what was necessary.

———

"Where did you go?" Tristan sat up on his bunk and leaned on one elbow.

"I told you." Turning my back to him, I shut the bunkroom door. "Out."

"Not good enough."

I scowled at him over my shoulder. "Who made you my keeper?"

"Stevens did, that's who." He swung his feet over the edge and then hopped to the floor. "Remember that?"

"No."

"Well, guess what? He did. So where'd you go?"

I stared at him for three full breaths and then brushed past him. Like this night hadn't already been horrible. Bowing my head so I wouldn't knock it on the bunk above mine, I dropped onto my bed. Eliza's eyes, hot with anger and moist with disappointment, flashed through my mind. I wished she had slapped me. Would make the fact that I'd crushed her easier to shoulder. But not Eliza. She was too perfect.

My chest burned. How could she not see that this was for her? How dare she accuse me of selfish ambitions?

"Here." Tristan bumped my shoulder with his fist.

I looked up, and a bottle of soda rested in his other hand. I glanced at his face, my eyebrows hiked.

"For peace, okay?" He pushed the drink toward me, and I took it. "I've got responsibilities, you know? People I have to answer to. That's all that was. No worries though. Okay?"

No worries? Not in this society. "Whatever." I took a long pull on the soda and let the fizz tickle my tongue. The sweet syrup begged for another go, and I emptied the bottle in three greedy gulps.

Are you safe now? Eliza's voice drifted like a haunting whisper in my mind. I stared at my hands. No. Not safe. No one was safe. Not out there, not in the Den. We were all one snitch away from becoming LiteRail cargo or public examples. I shivered.

"You okay, man?" Tristan crossed his arms and cocked his head.

"Fine." I shifted so I could stand. The room spun in circles. Setting my weight back against the mattress, I squeezed my eyes shut against the swirling image. The dizzying movement continued inside my head.

"Braxton?" Tristan's voice seemed to move away from me, echoing as though he'd spoken through a long tube.

I'm fine. Did I say that, or just think it? Was I fine?

"Come on. Let's go."

Go where? Were we going somewhere? The world shifted. Lights changed intensity, and then darkness smothered the light. Colors, harsh and vivid, jabbed my eyes. Rhythm pulsed into my ears, loud and overwhelming. Where were we?

"Here. Sit."

Good idea. Sitting would be good. I thought I sat. Or slumped. Voices swirled around me. Laughter ricocheted from every side. But over all of the flashing lights and noise, rhythm thudded like a heartbeat undergirding the chaos.

Red. Blue. Orange. Red again. Shadows passed between the bolts of color. Bodies colliding, shifting, separating, colliding again. My heart slowed, and I couldn't process the images my eyes took in. But I knew I shouldn't be there. Didn't want to be there, wherever there was.

Tristan.

He didn't answer. Did I call for him out loud, or had my mind misfired? I tried again. *Tristan.*

Shadows continued to slide around me, but none of them seemed to be him.

Get up and leave.

Misfired again. My numb brain couldn't connect with the rest of my body. Paralyzed. I'd been paralyzed. The realization hit me, and it should have wakened me from the fuzzy stupor, but even as panic jolted through my consciousness, my body continued to shut down. The shadows, the colors, the laughter, even the heartbeat of the room faded as I fell into a tunnel of black nothingness.

CHAPTER EIGHTEEN

"Braxton."

A large hand gripped the back of my neck and lifted.

"Braxton. Get up. Now."

A mild haze of consciousness trickled through my body. I peeled my eyes open only to find darkness beyond my lids.

The hand released my neck, but in the next moment there were two under my arms. "Shake it off, man. You can't get caught like this. They'll kill us."

Kill us? What did we do?

"Come. On." Arms locked around my chest from behind and tugged. "Now. Make your legs work. We need to leave right now."

I pushed my feet to the floor and hoped they'd hold my weight. The world swayed beneath me, but my legs didn't buckle.

"Good," said the voice behind me. Tristan. Pretty sure Tristan held me up. "Now, one foot in front of the other, buckaroo."

"Where are we?"

"Not now." He released my torso but kept a hand on my shoulder. "You're not gonna be able to put together walking and talking, so just focus on the walking until we get outside."

"But—" I stumbled, proving him right. With one hand, I caught myself on a table before my face planted into the floor. Instinctively, I orientated myself to the left. Because I knew this room like it'd been a second ho—

The Commons. Better known to me as the worship center. I hated the Commons. Told Tristan I didn't want to go. I snapped my posture straight and tried to whip around to face him. The room pulled out from under me. Tristan bear-hugged me from the side and set me upright again.

"Why am I here?"

"We're walking, Luther. Let's go. I told you—we're going to get in big trouble if you're caught like this."

"Like what?"

He pushed me forward. Fine. Outside. This conversation was going to happen though. I took three steps toward the double door exit leading to the main hall. Once again, Tristan's hand landed on my shoulder. "Not that way." He redirected me with another small shove toward the back of the room, stage left.

We passed the heavy curtains, which still hung from the tall ceiling, a remnant of the building's life as a church, and then entered a dark narrow hallway that led backstage and outside. A girl, maybe fifteen and shaved bald, huddled in the abandoned hall, covered by a Jackals coat. I glanced over to Tristan. No coat. Fire erupted in my stomach.

"She won't tell."

He thought that was what my glare was all about? I stopped, looked down at the Commons' provisional *entertainment*, and then back at Tristan.

"You're going to have to trust me on this, Luther." His eyes narrowed. "I'm not hurting her."

I launched forward, but my rubbery legs didn't carry any force. My attack fizzled as I flopped against him. He caught me by the shoulders and forced me vertical again. "Look. I get it," Tristan hissed near my ear. "You don't. Outside."

This time he wrapped a wad of my shirt in his fist and nearly dragged me to the back exit. Early-morning sunlight pierced my eyesight, and I was pretty sure it split my brain. I squeezed my eyes closed, and Tristan pushed me to the cold, wet grass.

"Breathe deep," he said, still standing. "Your head will clear in just a few minutes."

I cradled my searing skull in both hands, trying to make sense of the dark images my mind kept replaying. "What's going on?"

"You went to the Commons last night."

Uh, got that. With an attempt to ignore the sun's razor-sharp pain to my head, I looked up at him. "I told you I didn't want to."

"I persuaded you." Tristan crossed his arms but didn't look smug. He glanced around like a rabbit scanning the landscape for a predator. "You needed to go."

The soda. Tristan had given me a soda the night before, and then everything went screwy. "You drugged me?"

His lips pressed together.

I scowled, sitting up straight even though jolts of pain sparked inside my head. "Why?"

Tristan met my glare and didn't flinch. "Can you walk now?"

Could I pummel his face now?

He offered a hand, and I took it, doubling my other fist.

"Take it easy, Braxton." He pulled me to my feet. "I know more than you think, and you don't know nearly what you should."

———

Tristan inspected the landscape for the one-hundredth time before he tugged on the heavy metal door. The snow had melted, but the sloshy ground still bore the imprint of our boots. If someone wanted to track us, it wouldn't be that difficult. He guided the bald girl into the darkness and then stepped behind her.

I stopped, refusing to follow him through the door. "Why are we at the old factory?"

"Because it won't look suspicious."

I crossed my arms. "Sneaking into an abandoned factory won't look suspicious?"

"This was our hangout before the Jackals took over the church. Some of them still come here." He jerked his head in a *let's go* signal.

Come here for what? I looked to the girl. Pretty sure I didn't want to know. Not that I couldn't guess. Anger stiffened my muscles.

"What are you doing with her?"

Tristan held a hand up.

"No." I stepped through the door. "I want to know. Is she from the Uncloaked? What are—"

His arm came around my head, and his hand smacked over my mouth. "You talk too much, Braxton." He growled next to my ear. "Shut up until I know for sure we're safe."

With a decisive push, he sent me into the shadows and then stalked away with the girl, looking in all directions as he moved. I couldn't hear their footfalls until the staircase rattled in the far corner. They ascended, leaving me in the cold silence to replay the sultry images from the night before. Bald girls wearing a whole lot of not much. Had they been sealed? I tried to focus my memory on their necks. No tattoos. The haze in the room shrouded their faces, but terror palpitated from their stiff bodies.

My stomach heaved and emptied onto the cracked concrete. What kind of a society enslaved girls like that?

Desperately wicked...

I touched the ink embedded in my neck. It burned, forcing tears over my eyelids. *God, what have I done?* My eyes squeezed shut, and a tear dropped onto my chin. *I didn't know, God. Honest, I didn't. I just wanted to be safe. Wanted Eliza to be safe.*

"We're clear," Tristan said from the catwalk above the production floor.

He wasn't clear. Strength sprouted deep inside my chest and gained momentum with every step I took. He would not harm that girl. Wouldn't lay a hand on her.

I reached the top landing, spun on one foot, and then lunged into his chest. "You're disgusting. She's just a girl. A small, helpless girl!" My right fist connected with his jaw.

Tristan fell back but didn't crumble. With moves that had to have come from combat training, he caught both my wrists and then shoved me against the wall.

"Stop." He pulled me forward and then slammed me back again. "Stop and listen for once in your life, Luther. I'm not hurting her. As long as she has my coat, none of the other guys will touch her."

There were rules to this depravity?

"Look." His grip loosened but didn't fall. "I get it. You've got to hear me on this. I get it, Braxton, and you're right. It's the worst kind of horrible." His voice cracked on the last word, and his hands dropped.

Silence settled in the dimness of the abandoned factory, and I studied the guy in front of me. He was a bully. I'd seen it —watched him handle Kipper like a piece of rabbit meat. Saw him beat Mr. Elliot. Why would a kid like that have any concern whatsoever for a girl who, by Jackals standards, was apparently alive only to gratify his lusts?

"You don't know me." He turned so he was no longer facing me and then leaned against the wall by my side. "Do you?"

I rolled my head to look at him. "Tristan Melzner. Defensive lineman, three-year starter. And a snitch on the Uncloaked. Yeah, I know you."

He slid down to the floor, leaned his elbows against his knees, and stared at his boots. "I took the seal for the same reason you did."

Doubtful. He'd been sealed long before I had. Hadn't known the pleasures of feasting on watery broth and shivering through frigid winter nights. Losing his home. Watching his father tortured. No way he understood why I took the pledge. I worked my jaw and then sat on the floor next to him.

"I thought if I went with the tide, everything would be okay." His hands twisted and then locked together tight. "The Elliots? I threw up that night and then beat my fists against a brick wall until every knuckle bled. Didn't know Kipper, but it still killed me, what we did. I only did it because—"

Because they told him to? *Not feeling any pity here.* Silence stole the space again.

Tristan sniffed. "Hulk threatened my sister." He turned

his eyes to me, and his gaze bore into mine. Agony. A soul tortured stared back at me.

"I thought that if I were sealed, they'd leave my family alone. Think that happened?" Anger hardened his voice. "They shipped them out two weeks after the Elliots. Do you know what happens in Reformation Camp?"

My jaw trembled, and I held my lips together with my teeth. *God, I don't want to know.*

Tristan's stare grew vacant, cold. "You'll learn soon enough." He looked away and tipped his head back against the wall. "I know you saw Eliza last night. I'm supposed to keep tabs on you. I took you to the Commons so that you'd be seen there. I didn't want to have to explain why you were gone."

I clenched my hands together, trying to quell the shivers that covered my body. "Thanks." The word caught in my throat.

His eyes turned to me again, and the weight of his stare settled onto my consciousness. "You can't ever see her again, Braxton."

Like the slab of iron on the table that had pressed the life out of my father, his words clamped over my heart. Pain wasn't a strong enough word. My forehead fell against my fists. "I know."

The girl down the hall shifted, drawing my attention. "Who is she?"

Tristan shrugged. "Her name is Miranda. That's all I know."

"Is she from Glennbrooke?"

"No."

I twisted my hands together and swallowed. "What will happen to her?"

Tristan leaned back, letting the back of his head tap against the steel wall. "They cycle them through—they stay for about a week, their last chance to submit to the Party before...they're shipped back to the Purge."

I closed my eyes against the sting of our shameful reality. "The Purge... What is that?" Another question I really didn't want answered.

"What do you think?" His voice steamed with indignant fury. "*If they cannot reform, they must be purged.* What do you think that means?"

I swallowed around a hard, painful lump. Misery draped in our silence. *Are you safe?* No, Eliza. No one was safe. Satan had gripped our nation, and his minions ravaged our people. And the horror of it all? The American people shut their eyes to reality. They didn't know, because they didn't want to know.

I didn't want to know.

A little-girl whimper pierced through my chest.

"You can't let them." I clenched my jaw and set a determined stare on Tristan. "She has your coat. She's under your protection. You can do something."

Tristan sat up and scowled. "What am I going to do?" His eyes set hard on me, though his chin quivered. "Do you know how many I've tried to protect? Got a number, Luther?"

My eyebrows came together. Did this matter?

"Eight." His voice broke. "Eight girls, exactly Anniah's age. And every one of them gets herded onto that railcar and sent to their deaths. Do you know what I can do about that? Nothing. Nothing! Don't think for a minute in that pious head of yours that that doesn't rot in my gut every waking day of my life. You don't know. You've only just begun this nightmare, so you don't know."

The tenor of his voice vibrated the iron catwalk beneath

us. Quiet descended again, and with it a new darker shade of black.

"Anniah..." I whispered. "Your sister?"

"Yeah." His head dropped almost between his knees.

"Did she..."

"Purged." The lifeless vacancy in his voice sent a chill over my skin. "Handled by Hulk and then sent to the Purge. I could do nothing."

My eyes burned. I glanced over to Tristan. Tears dripped off his nose. I looked away, trying to control the trembling in my jaw.

"What will you do with her?" I whispered, looking back at the girl.

"Protect her while she's here." He ran a hand over his hair and then pulled his head down, as if he were covering it in shame. "That's all I can do."

I sat up straighter. "No. We can get her out. I know a place—"

"We can't." His voice, already low, dropped to a barely audible whisper. "They track them. Even if I could hide her, smuggle her away, they would find her, and her death would be unbelievably painful."

Hopelessness slithered around me, wrapping an invisible but icy grip around my neck and squeezing. The image that fear always pulled to my mind surfaced with perfect clarity. Eliza.

Not my Eliza.

CHAPTER NINETEEN

Light began to touch Main Street as I walked through the park. Morning drills would be at the gym today—our token day off to earn our undying gratitude and loyalty. Who signed up for this stuff? I mean, without having been bullied into it?

The steel table still loomed in the middle of the park—the Progressive's ever-present threat chilling any hotheaded rebel. People only needed to look at the tilted torture device, and they could picture my father's dead body crushed between the iron clamps. Or maybe that was just me.

Staring at the place of his murder made my head light and blurred the world around me, but my attention continued to drift back to the table anyway. Why did I come here? I had nowhere else to go, and as I began to peel back the layers of resentment that had kept me from my father, I realized how much I needed him. Then. Now. I needed his wisdom, his resolve.

My chin quivered, and I clenched my jaw. I'd managed to

get myself in the thick of something massive and ugly and darker than the blackest cave. What would I do? Could I do? The Hadleys were next. I didn't know them, but it didn't matter. All I knew was that they were next on the hit list, and their three small children...

Tristan's words pierced me with both a sharp grief and a new, bold, and poignant anger. Revelation is power, and now I knew. I saw what they did to the Uncloaked—to their innocent girls whose spines had outlasted the Party's threats. And I'd been warned what they would do to the children who belonged to rebel families.

Indignation flared in my chest. How dare they? How dare the Party rip apart families? Who gave them the right to *intervene* in the home lives of those who would not bow to their will?

We did. The flame within sputtered, died back, and pooled into something much worse. Shame. Suddenly my father's voice touched my hearing. *Apathy is the illness of the overpriviliged.* A lethal disease. One that took its victim and ravished every member of its frame until only ugly deformities remained.

We did this. Because we did nothing.

Misery sank into my stomach, turning up a sour indigestion. I walked to the nearest oak and leaned my back against it, breathing in the cool spring air as if it could purge the sickness gripping my insides.

Something caught my eye in the gray predawn shadows. A movement across from the park, beyond the street. I followed the depression in the vacant area. Nothing. But there had been something. Someone.

Near the pharmacy.

My stomach knotted with a knowledge my eyes couldn't confirm. I pushed away from the tree, checking to my left and then to my right. The town held in quiet stillness as it waited for the day to begin. Crossing the grass, I cut south, past the parallel spot where Evan Knight's business lay. Further south, because I didn't want suspicion cast upon my direction by anyone whom I might not see.

After crossing the street, I began to trot down the sidewalk that ran perpendicular and two blocks south of the pharmacy. If she were going back, she'd stick to the alleyways. I passed the first building on the block, the clinic, and then ducked into the narrow passage that separated it from the postal distribution center behind it. Night still gripped the area where street-lamps didn't threaten its reign, and I pressed my back against the brick of the clinic until my eyes adjusted.

To my right, the shadows shifted again—definitely a person. A small dark-haired person, whose tiny frame made my heart nearly explode as anxiety throbbed in my veins. She crept down the way toward me, and my teeth sank into my bottom lip until the metal taste of blood oozed onto my tongue.

I stepped from the profile of the building, certain that she would see my movement. She froze and then huddled against the opposite building. Only half a block away, she wouldn't have a chance. What was she thinking?

As if a gun had gone off for an Olympic sprint, I darted forward. She spun and ran, her dark hair flowing behind her. She didn't make it to the end of the block before I caught a wrist.

"Please," she sobbed. She twisted her arm, trying to wrench it out of my grip. "Please—"

I slid a hand over her mouth. "Liza, stop."

My face near hers, I could make out her terrified expression. Fear pulsed in her shaking limbs, and panic blazed in those innocent eyes.

"It's me, Liza." I pushed my free hand into her hair and pulled her head against my shoulder.

For a moment she stiffened, pushing against my chest, but in the next breath she buried her face against me and fisted my coat. "How could you do that to me?" Her whisper quaked.

I blocked the way her fear probed at my vulnerability. This wasn't a game. "What are you doing here?" I pulled away and leaned down to her face. "I told you to stay away."

"My mother is sick. Pneumonia."

I gripped her shoulder, tempted to shake her. "Your mother is sick? Eliza, what if someone other than me saw you? What if Hulk had you in his grip right now? You've got to listen to me—"

"She's dying, Braxton." A cry fractured her voice. "I can't sit there and watch my mother die."

Tension drained from my arms, and my shoulders slumped. "Where's your dad?"

"Back at the cellar. They don't know I came."

So Eliza. Nothing in the world would stop her from following her convictions. I stared at her, knowing with sudden clarity that I loved her. Not love like I love a good sparring, or love like I loved my mother's lasagna. I *loved* this girl, and I was equally certain that if the Party took her, sent her away, and... I couldn't complete that scenario. I'd die. I'd curl up into a pathetic waste of a human and die.

I gripped both of her shoulders. "Liza, you have to get sealed." Heat filled my voice, and I squeezed her shoulders. "I need you to do this."

She shrank in my hold and stared at me wide eyed. "I can't."

There was a fine line between passion and anger, one that at that moment, I couldn't distinguish. My fingers sank into her arms, and I hovered over her with a demanding stance. "No. That's not good enough now. I know what they do, and I can't let that happen. You have to get sealed."

Her eyes closed, and a whimper left her mouth. "You're hurting me."

What was I doing? Ice poured over me, and I unclasped my hands. "I'm sorry." I pushed a hand through my hair and then rubbed my face. "I'm so sorry, Liza." I couldn't look at her. I disappointed her, scared her, and now hurt her. What kind of guy did that?

Jackal.

Bile burned my throat. God, please don't let me be that guy.

Eliza's hand wrapped around my arm, sliding down the length of it until she reached my hand and then into my palm. Her fingers wove into mine, and she squeezed. "I know, Braxton."

Her voice beckoned me, and I looked at her. How does such a small person embody such enormous grace? I studied her face as the light began to chase away the darkness. Her soft brown eyes, full of kindness and yet anchored with solid determination. A light spray of freckles that had faded over the winter. Her mouth.

I stopped there and fixed my gaze back on hers. Surely she must have known what I was thinking—feeling—but her stare didn't waver or flicker with fear. I lowered my forehead against hers, and she tilted her chin so our noses brushed.

With my free hand, I rubbed my thumb along her jawline. "Liza, I need you. You're all I have left. Please—"

She moved just enough so her lips met mine. I answered

her kiss with one of my own. What did this mean? Was she saying she would concede—take the pledge and accept the seal? Questions filled my mind and then vanished as I gave in to the sensation of her mouth against mine. I shifted into a cerebral numbness and allowed my senses to rule the moment. Adrenaline rushed through my core and spread through my limbs. Every nerve tingled, came alive, and rejoiced.

Eliza backed away, pulling the fog of pleasure with her. I swallowed, trying to calm the rambunctious thudding of my heart and regain a steady breath. The questions returned, and I studied her face, hoping to read an answer in her expression. She must have read mine.

"You know I can't do that." Her hand cupped my face, fingers fanning over my cheek. She pressed one more kiss against my mouth. "Not even for you."

A tear slipped over her eyelid, and she moved as if to escape. With my palm on her face, I held her in place and brushed the drop of dew from her cheek. This moment...my lungs felt useless, and my heart surged with painful strength. The best and worst moment I'd shared with my best friend. Images pushed into my mind—Miranda, my father—threatening panic into my chest.

I would lose her either way. Tristan had been right—I shouldn't see her. Every moment I spent with her stamped another target on her precious soul. Hulk had even indicated that he'd come after her—if I didn't fall in line. There was an *if* in that implied threat, wasn't there? But to lose her by way of a Reformation Camp and maybe the Purge? Terror clamped hard on my heart. Unacceptable.

She shifted again, her body drifting away. "I have to go."

Her hand slid over mine, and she gently tugged my palm from her cheek. I curled my fingers over hers and let my knuckles trail over the outline of her face. Squeezing my hand, she took two steps away.

"Liza." I stopped her retreat, refusing to let go. "Meet me tonight, in the woods down by the hose factory."

The soft morning light slid between the buildings, touching her face as she lifted a small smile. With another squeeze on my fingers, she slipped into the shadows of the cross alley.

God, keep her safe, because I can't.

I watched the dark path long after she disappeared from view.

Maybe there was a way I could.

———

"What did you use on me to get me to go to the Commons?"

Tristan didn't look at me, just continued to tie the laces on his boots. "Nothing. You went to the Commons all on your own."

I looked around the bunk room. Empty. I had made sure everyone had gone before I asked. Scowling, I turned back to him. His hard stare met mine.

"Are you going tonight?" he asked, an eyebrow cocked as if to say going wasn't optional.

"Yeah." I pushed off my bunk. "I'm going. After I check the factory." Maybe this was a game of covert intentions. If I could read his unspoken language, maybe he could read mine, and we'd both stay out of the Jackals crosshairs.

Tristan nodded. "I'm taking Miranda there."

Before or after he went to the Commons? Not a safe question.

"How about you?"

A vile film coated the inside of my throat. I knew what he meant, but saying things like that, coating his intent with that kind of inhuman crassness, still made me sick. "No. I'm going alone."

"Alone? By choice?" Tristan turned his back to me. "Maybe you need to persuade someone."

I pulled my eyebrows together. What was he hinting at? He turned back around, a bottle of water clasped in his fist. "Bet you're not thirsty now, but there's nothing available down at the factory." He pushed the bottle toward me. "Take it, in case you need it."

Persuasion. Did he know what I had been working toward earlier?

He stepped toward the door but paused before he left. His chin moved into his shoulder, as if he were going to cough. "Consider the costs." He cleared his throat, and his serious eyes connected with mine.

The room held in a cold silence—a wake of responsibility left by his somber warning. He must know. I had no doubt he'd seen Eliza that morning. But why the warning? He agreed with me, didn't he? Wouldn't he have done the same with his sister if he could go back?

I stared at the bottle. Clear, nonthreatening. Persuasion's danger lay invisible. *Count the cost.* She'd hate me. I might hate myself. But seeing her herded onto a LiteRail car would kill me.

Snagging my backpack from the foot of my bunk, I closed my eyes and replayed the early hours of morning. In a world that had turned dark and terrifying, Eliza's kiss had been warm and sweet. She was my sun in this nightmare. My anchor. How could I let harm come to her when I had the power to stop it?

But...how could I strip her of her soul?

The battle continued in my mind as I slipped the strap of my bag over my shoulder. The April days had grown longer, but I needed to leave the Den now if I wanted to reach the factory before dusk settled. I'd stay there until evening's quilt blanketed the land. Maybe by then I would know what to do.

CHAPTER TWENTY

I PUSHED FARTHER SOUTH OF THE FACTORY BEFORE I stepped into the woods. The more distance from town, the better, and it was the opposite direction of the Knights' shelter. This was stupid and dangerous all on its own, and the last thing I wanted was to draw a map for the Jackals. Weaving through the trees, the damp smell of deteriorating leaves and muddy earth filled my nose. I kept my hands up, palms out, and passed from tree to tree as the rough bark guided me deeper in.

Click, click...click.

I waited, hoping she heard me and had her internal GPS up and running. Using our call borderlined insanity, and I didn't want to do it more than once. Leaning my head against a tree, I held my breath. A small animal scurried some distance in front of me, its quick movements rustling against the damp leaves. The air above me moved, and a branch creaked before a pair of wings beat against the dark. Nature's nighttime symphony—hopefully it covered Eliza and me.

Click, click...click.

I cringed. She wasn't far, but every sound we made was like a ping against a sonar, and I didn't know who, if anyone, was out there. With silent steps, I moved toward the spot of her sound. One tree, then two. Five...seven, eight. A hand brushed mine as I tagged the ninth stride.

"I'm here." Her whisper floated on the air. "Come on." She gripped the hand I had brushed the bark with and pulled me in the dark.

With the deftness of a nocturnal animal, she wove into the sanctuary of protection. The ground began to change beneath my feet. Soft dirt interrupted by veins of roots and sapling shoots became solid, craggy, and colder. A slope began to draw my weight downward, and I braced against the pull. Our motion became more side step than forward as the sound of rushing water replaced the chorus of birds and mice.

"It's slick," Eliza whispered as she released my hand.

I used both palms to brace myself against the angled rocks. Eliza moved quickly, as if she'd been a mountain goat at some point in her childhood. Where were we? And how did she know where to go?

"Here." Her hand clasped mine again and tugged me into the rock.

Except there wasn't rock right there. The air nipped and smelled of frozen water as a new shade of black dropped over my eyes.

"Keep your back to the mill wall and take five side steps, then feel behind you. There'll be an opening."

I clung to her hand and followed her lead. Five steps, and the wall at my back disappeared. She guided me ten steps deeper, and a light pierced the darkness. I shut my eyes as the intrusion jarred my senses. Blinking, my surroundings slowly registered in my brain. Ancient boards lined a room that had been dug underground.

"Where are we?"

"At an old mill from another century." Her breath filtered in white puffs through the LED light she held in her hand.

"When did you start playing archeologist?" I whispered, still afraid of the things I could not see.

"When I became an enemy of the state."

I shivered, looking at her tiny frame. Smaller than I remembered. "Are you hungry?"

A tiny laugh escaped her mouth. "Do birds fly?"

The corners of my mouth tipped up. How could she do that? Starving, the little bird could still chirp like morning had just dawned, making me smile.

I leaned against the solid wall behind us and slid down until my backside hit the damp ground. Eliza followed me, and I unzipped my pack. Digging inside, I found an orange and handed it to her. Her eyes rounded like I'd just pulled out the most beautiful diamond she'd ever seen.

"Oh"—she smelled it—"fruit." Her eyes closed, and she smiled.

What were they living on? I wished my offering had been more, not the simple leftovers I'd tucked away after drills this morning.

Her dirty fingers trembled as she tore a section away and slipped it into her mouth. "Mmm." She leaned her forehead against my shoulder. "So good."

So sad. I wished I could do better for her. Bring her something more fitting to her noble character.

She sniffed, and her hands continued to shake.

"Are you cold?"

Another slice went into her mouth, and she shrugged. I

shifted so I could pull my arms from the sleeves of my coat. Eliza scowled at the emblem embroidered on the chest as I raised the jacket to drape over her shoulders.

"It's just a coat, Liza. You don't have to keep it."

A grin peeked onto her lips, and I settled my jacket around her petite frame. Only her hands poked out, and I moved again so I could wrap both arms around her. She leaned back against me, and I tightened my hold.

Water leaked into the corner of the mill and dripped in our silence, the *plop, plop, plop* set against the background of the rushing creek outside. Eliza continued to poke bites into her mouth as she rested in my arms.

I pressed a kiss to her hair and then laid a cheek on top of her head. "Are your parents okay?"

"For the moment." Fear tainted her voice.

"Your mom?"

"Still wheezing."

Not good.

She finished eating and tucked her hands inside the coat. I rubbed her arms, willing warmth into her skin.

"Braxton, there's more Uncloaked at the cellar." She moved so she could tilt her face up to mine. "It's not just us now."

"How did they find you?"

"There are people scattered throughout the forest. Hiding. Starving." She paused and swallowed. "And there are whispers."

Alarm buzzed in my head. What was she leading up to?

She held my gaze. "They say there's a place, a refuge. Somehow, they've cut themselves off from the government, and the Party can't reach them, or doesn't know about them."

"A rebel community?"

She nodded.

"Sounds like a fairy tale, Liza."

"Maybe." She ducked her head and then snuggled deeper into my chest. "I'd rather think of it as hope." One hand peeked out of the coat and trailed against my arm. "They're organizing a group to go."

Warning flared into full-fledged panic. I sat up. "You're not going, are you?"

Her sigh blew warmth against my chest. I wanted to capture it and tape it to my heart. "Not now. Mom is still too sick. But we can't stay..."

No, they couldn't. How long before the Party would begin raiding the forest, hunting for their elusive prey? No doubt Eliza Knight was at the top of that list. The Jackals didn't know her parents were still alive, but Eliza? She'd be another trophy for the Progressive propaganda.

Miranda's shallow face, her hollow, lifeless eyes, pushed back into my memory. I couldn't let that happen to Eliza.

My attention drifted to my pack, settling on the water bottle I'd secured in the side pouch. My gut swirled painfully. She'd hate me. But if she knew what was out there, what godless, heartless people did to the Uncloaked, maybe...

Maybe she'd forgive me.

CHAPTER TWENTY-ONE

A GIRL'S SCREAM SHATTERED THE NIGHT AIR, redirecting my resolve. Eliza seemed to push away from me and stand all in one motion. I pulled my hand from the bottle I'd grasped and jumped to my feet. With her flashlight pointed toward the exit, she moved to leave. I wrapped a hand around her elbow and pulled her back.

"You can't go out there." With two steps, I slid around her and blocked her route.

Her back stiffened. "What if it's one of the Uncloaked?"

"I'll go." I took the light from her fingers. "No one knows about this place. No one knows you're here. Stay."

Like she ever did that when I told her to. I caught an arched eyebrow as I turned away. Should have tried to reason with her again, but the decibel of that scream still throbbed in my ears.

I ducked around the corner of the mill and searched for the opening Eliza had brought me through. In the path of light, I could make out a sagging doorframe surrounded by buckled wood planks. The relic was ready to collapse—a death trap waiting for a decent gust of wind. What had Eliza been thinking?

We'd discuss her lack of judgment later. I stooped through the ready-to-collapse construction and scrambled up the wet rock bank. Once I breached the top, I stopped and looked down at what remained of the mill, imagining how Liza and I had sat inside. We'd been facing east. That put whoever had screamed north, toward town.

The hairs on my arms stood at attention, and I clamped my jaw. A Jackal wouldn't scream like that—he wouldn't have a reason to. But an Uncloaked...so many reasons to pitch terror into the night.

I doubled my fist. Ignoring the cry wasn't an option. If I didn't go see what happened, Eliza would. Not gonna happen.

I picked my way through the brush, finding travel tremendously easier with a light. I wondered how close to the creek we had walked earlier, and thinking of it gave me a chill. The water moved faster here, and the walls guiding the flow were solid rock. One wrong step and we would have been in trouble. How had Eliza acquired night vision?

Leaves rustled somewhere in front of me. I stopped, clicking off my light. Mice again? Only if they were really, really big. My heart kicked into a new gear, and I worked to quell my rapid breath.

A whimper sounded from a tree ten feet from me. Swallowing, I crept forward, counting my steps. One, two, three... My muscles locked into fight-ready mode. Eight, nine...

"Help."

Did I imagine that wispy voice?

"Please." It came a little louder, but quivered. "Please, help."

With my thumb, I snapped my light on, but rather than shining it toward the girl's voice, I swept the area around us.

"It's just me," she whispered. "He said you would find me —that you would help me."

Wait, what? I turned the light on her. She ducked away from exposure, her eyes squeezing against the beam. The glow of the LED bulb bounced off her shaved head as she huddled into a muddy blanket.

I gulped in a breath. "Miranda, right?"

Her head moved against the fabric. I could only stare. What had Tristan done?

A presence behind me disturbed the air, and my muscles tensed again. Whipping around, light in hand, I flashed the beam down the path I'd just come.

Shouldn't have been surprised.

"Eliza," I ground between my teeth. She jogged the remaining two yards to us. I glared at her. "You are so stubborn."

She cocked her head. "Learned from the champ." Her eyes shifted from me to the girl huddled next to the tree, and her sassy expression withered. "Do you know her?"

I turned the flashlight back in the general direction where Miranda stood but kept the force of the light directed to the ground. Her dignity had already been stripped. Seemed like I could give her a least a little bit of respect.

"Her name is Miranda. That's all I know."

Miranda managed to look at Eliza without really moving her head. "Can you help me?"

Eliza put a hand to her shoulder but looked at me. "Uncloaked?"

"Yes." I swallowed. How was I going to explain this to

Eliza? Heat crept over my skin. "From a Reformation Camp. She's here—she's been sentenced to the Purge."

I didn't know if Eliza knew what that meant. She was smart though—didn't take more than a second to figure it out, and she nodded.

"What happened?"

Miranda pulled the blanket tighter around her shoulders. "He cut out my tag."

"Tristan?" I asked.

Eliza's round eyes bounced from Miranda to me. "Tristan? Tristan, the guy who ratted on Kipper Elliot, Tristan?"

Miranda's head came up. "He said he would help me." She pushed her chin at me. "He said—"

"Wait," Eliza said. "Tristan cut out your tag? Where was your tag?"

Miranda turned forty-five degrees and rested her chin on her shoulder. "Here, behind the bone so we can't reach them."

Without a pause, Eliza tugged on Miranda's elbow. "You're bleeding then. Come on."

Yeah, I should have thought about that. But this was big. Tristan had freed an Uncloaked, a girl destined for the Purge. An act of treason. And he put me, and Eliza, in the middle of it. Was he for real—or was he setting me up?

I followed the girls as Eliza cut a quick path back to the mill, my mind working as if I'd been given a trig problem. Except trig problems didn't typically involve death. Why didn't Tristan stay with Miranda? He'd followed me tonight. Why didn't he just bring her into the mill and give us a rundown of his plan?

What exactly was his plan?

Some kind of male instinct kicked in, and I braced Miranda as we scurried down the creek bank. Without glancing around, Eliza darted into the opening and led the way through the dilapidated building until we reached the spot where my pack still lay.

"Here." With a firm hand, Eliza directed Miranda to the ground and peeled the blanket away from the wound. She didn't pause at Miranda's near nakedness, nor did she flinch at the sight of blood oozing from a blade wound two inches long. "Braxton, I need your shirt. Do you have water?"

Water, yes. But only one bottle she could use. The other...

My gaze settled on Eliza. Never once did the girl think about what helping Miranda would cost, which, in fact, could be her life. Wouldn't matter if it crossed her mind anyway. I fingered the spot where my seal rested under my collar. I had counted the costs and had come up short. What had I almost done to Eliza?

Inking her would have killed her on the inside. I'd been minutes away from murdering my best friend's soul. I felt myself shrinking, my breath catching hard in my lungs.

"Braxton, I really need something to put pressure on this cut." Eliza glanced over her shoulder at me. "Your shirt? Something? It's a clean laceration, but I think it's deep. Can you help me out?"

Nobility had somehow skipped over me. Somewhere in the process of growing up, resenting my dad and coveting the life I thought I'd deserved, gallantry had been choked out and left for dead. Except when it came to Eliza.

What if what she saw in me could be true for real?

I tugged both my sweater and my T-shirt off. The early-spring night air wrapped me with its icy fingers, and my torso became one giant goose bump. Eliza tugged the T-shirt free and passed my sweater back, her hand brushing my arm as she moved. Must be what a frozen field feels like when a sun beam breaks through the clouds and warms a spot of soil.

But I didn't linger there. "What else?" I asked Eliza, wanting more than anything in that moment to prove her faith in me true. "Tell me what to do."

"Hold the light." She lifted her flashlight off the floor where she'd positioned it facing upward and handed it to me. "I need to see how deep it is." After she settled on her knees, she drew a calm breath and began speaking softly to Miranda. "Tell us about this tag. What's it do?"

"It's how they keep us." Miranda shivered enough to shake the blanket she kept tight around her lower arms. "Like a shock collar for a dog, only embedded where we can't get to it, and near enough to our hearts that the right amount of voltage sent through it will kill us."

The light I held bounced under the unsteadiness of my hand. Treated like dogs. This was how we dealt with people who would not comply. I focused on Eliza, afraid that my anger would snap.

Eliza examined Miranda's wound, her face drawn tight and her scowl telling.

"What can you do about it?" I whispered, wishing Miranda couldn't hear the hopelessness in my voice.

Eliza bit her bottom lip. That meant nothing. She couldn't do anything, no matter how deep the wound was.

"Maybe there's something back at the cellar I can use to stitch it up." She glanced at me. "Can you help me get her back there?"

"No." Miranda, who hadn't even moaned as Eliza fingered the gash, looked over her shoulder at the two of us. "Tristan said you have to get back. You have to go to the Commons."

I frowned. "I thought he said I was supposed to help you."

"And you have." She lifted her chin, and I watched as her eyes communicated gratitude. "He said you knew someone who would take care of me. Now you have to go back."

"She's right." Eliza nodded, and her gaze fell on me. "They'll know you were involved once they find out she's missing, unless you go back."

Eliza wanted me back in the Den? "You said I'd be safe. We'd be safe. Thirty minutes ago, you wanted me to leave the Jackals."

"Thirty minutes ago I didn't know this." She tipped her head toward Miranda.

Somehow my chest shrunk and my shoulders grew all at the same time. She could make a hero out of a mouse. Or a cockroach. "Liza, it's not—"

Twisting on her knees, she turned so that she was parallel to me and slipped her frozen hands into mine. Her eyes bore into me, and in the hypnotic power of that gaze, I began to believe her thoughts before she even gave them voice. I could be who she saw, the guy she always had believed me to be.

"It's like Esther." Hope overcame the dreary discouragement that had become standard in her eyes. "Not completely, but think about it, Braxton. She was in the palace of a king who didn't belong to her people. Do you remember what Mordecai said to her?"

I chuckled as I tightened my hold on her hands. "Quotes are your department."

Her lopsided smile made me think of warm summer days by the creek under our oak. I didn't feel the chilly air anymore. "He said that she was there for such a time as this." She bit her lip, which had suddenly begun to tremble. "To save her people."

A quiver took hold in my chest. I'd never realized how

terrifying it was to become someone's hope—her hero. "I'm *not* a noble person, Eliza."

Her smile turned soft and tender, and her thumb brushed over my knuckles. "Some are born great, some achieve greatness, and some have greatness thrust upon them."

Something emerged inside of me, like the real me—the one who'd been stuffed away and wrapped tight by anger and selfishness—he broke free. Grew and took over. I mashed my lips together and closed my eyes. "Another quote?"

"William Shakespeare."

I slipped my hands from hers so that I could frame her face with my palms. I leaned toward her until our noses touched. "You are my greatness," I whispered and then brushed her lips with mine.

She covered my hands with hers. "Someday you'll know, Braxton. You'll see. Everything that I see is inside you... God made you to be this man. It's not because of me." She grazed my mouth once more and then pulled away to turn back toward Miranda. "Now go. Follow the creek until you can see the light from the rail station. Turn right as soon as you see it, and you'll be able to find the factory."

I drank in a long breath, willing the courage that had just blossomed to take firm root in my heart, and then stood.

"Braxton?" Eliza's voice caught me as I turned to leave. "One more quote."

"Okay."

"You have to hang on to this one, all right?"

"Okay."

"Promise?"

I laughed. "Okay, Liza. I promise. Tell me."

"To go against one's conscience is neither right nor safe."

Silence settled in the mill as I repeated her words in my

mind. It was what she'd been trying to tell me all along. "Who said that?"

Her smile tipped toward the ornery sort, and she shrugged. "You have his name." She turned back to her patient. "I guess you'll have to figure it out."

Not hard. Martin Luther had been near the top of my father's hero list. I didn't know he'd said anything that... profound though.

"Will you remember?" Eliza asked.

"I'll remember." I walked away.

Without my pack.

CHAPTER TWENTY-TWO

SURVIVING THE COMMONS HAD NEARLY CRUSHED EVERY fiber of my moral being. It had been better going when I was drugged. Was all of the depravity really okay—embraced—by everyone there? *Be careful, little eyes, what you see...*where had that gone?

I had made eye contact with Tristan at some point during my obligatory appearance. He held my look long enough so I knew he'd seen me, but communicated nothing in that glance. I couldn't figure him, and it made me edgy. Why would he set Miranda free if he wasn't opposed to the Jackals—to the Party? But why would he leave me hanging if he was actually dissenting from the Den?

Changing after our morning workout, I let worry flood my mind. I'd never imagined the danger I had found myself swimming in. Check a box—save your life? How had I been so simpleminded? Now I was in the den of the enemy, committing treason right under their noses, and at any moment my partner in crime could rat me out. Worse, he could disclose

Eliza's whereabouts and turn her in for not only defiance but treason.

"Better start moving, Luther." Tristan startled me, ripping me out of the terror in my mind and bringing me back to the nightmare I'd signed up for. "Classes in five."

"What if I don't go?"

He arched an eyebrow. "Is that a real question?"

I drew in a breath and squared my shoulders. "Are you threatening me?"

Tristan stared at me for two full breaths. "Be smart, Braxton. Just be smart."

His tone gave nothing away. I couldn't read the things he wasn't saying, and it spun a web of anxiety in my brain.

"It's just social equalities class." He turned away and snagged his tab from the shelf by our bunk. "Go. Participate. Blend."

Was there a message in that?

I went. I participated. I blended. If we weren't living under a government that demanded total loyalty or death, you'd think it was a day in the life of a normal seventeen-year-old. *God, please don't let this be the new normal.*

We had a break after lunch. A whole hour all to myself so I could sort through the tangled chaos I'd jumped into. I walked to Main and ended up at the park, staring at the spot where my father had been martyred. The choices I'd made since then rolled through my head, each one a new failure to add to the growing stack of *Braxton's pile of foolishness.* Instead of gaining freedom, I'd surrendered to total bondage. Instead of protecting Eliza, I'd put her in greater danger. And now...

For such a time as this.

Eliza's gentle voice drifted into my mind, calming the whirlwind of all my inadequacies. I was a sellout. She saw opportunity. I was weak. She beckoned a new kind of strength. *God, can this be so?* How could she see greatness in my spinelessness? How could she be sure that I was here, a Jackal, for such a time as this?

Miranda's sad face passed through my memory. One life saved. Eliza would say it was worth it, no matter what the cost. But as of that moment, we hadn't been caught. Cost was irrelevant when you didn't really have to pay.

Shouting diverted my attention, snagging my gaze toward the south end of Main. A crowd gathered at the LiteRail, peppered with the green coats of the Jackals. Another cargo load. My chest caved, and the familiar nausea started to swirl in my gut. Didn't people understand what was happening? Did they not know what Reformation Camps were?

Had I? Not really. Not the full extent—and I probably still didn't know. There were things that the Party kept hidden, and they did it well. They kept us happy with handouts. Busy with our own comfy lives. Satisfied with the glossy, the superficial. Distracted and unaware.

Why would anyone living a normal life know the dark reality of unchecked evil? The average American ate, slept, went to work and school, came home, and watched Party-approved television. How were they supposed to know?

Drawn to the commotion, I moved southward down Main. My stomach growled, despite feeling sick, reminding me that I hadn't eaten lunch. Wait, lunch? Something was off. Raids didn't happen until after our classes were complete—waiting until evening made it easier to catch a rebellious family together. Optimal herding tactics. I cringed. Why were they sending someone now?

Alarm—no total panic—zipped through my veins. Searching the gathering, I willed the crowd to split. Like a squirming worm, the group wiggled and shifted, and for a brief moment, their movement allowed me a glimpse.

I stopped breathing. *God, no. Please, please, no.*

My feet carried me at a sprint, faster than I'd ever run in football. From my left, another pair of pounding feet sounded behind me, and I was vaguely aware of Tristan on my heels.

"Braxton." He snagged my arm and yanked me back toward a building.

I pushed him away and turned. With all of his power-packed lineman muscles, he wrestled me to the ground. "Don't. You don't want to go there."

"What did you do?" I swung, and my fist landed against his jaw. He tipped back, probably more from surprise than from force, and I wriggled to my feet. My heart throbbed painfully as I pushed my legs faster, but nothing was going to stop me.

"Eliza!" I dove into the crowd, blindly shoving aside whoever stood between me and her.

Suddenly the commotion stopped and the crowd seemed to part. She stood on the loading platform, her hands bound together at her back. A hateful red mark bulged on one cheekbone, the imprint of knuckles screaming with purple fury.

"Well, Luther." Hulk stood behind her, his gorilla fist locked on her hair. "Where have you been? I was sure I'd find you two together."

My eyes darted from his snarled face to hers. A trickle of blood ran from the corner of her mouth. The mouth I had just kissed not twenty-four hours before. The mouth that had spoken hope and life to my beaten soul. I blinked, and the tears burned inside my eyelids.

"Eliza," I whispered, "what happened?"

She licked the side of her mouth that wasn't bleeding but didn't respond.

"We're missing a girl, Luther." Hulk yanked on her hair. "Know anything about that?"

My gaze didn't leave hers.

"Luther!" Hulk released his hold and then pushed her aside as he launched my direction. "I asked you a question."

"Easy, Lieutenant." Another familiar voice spoke from behind me, and steps accompanied his speech. I broke my stare from Eliza to see Jedidiah stride up beside Hulk. "Braxton was at the Commons last night and in class today. He's not on trial here."

I looked back to Eliza, and my lips parted to speak, but she shook her head, her eyes pleading in the silence.

"Fine," Hulk growled. "But this girl is guilty. Uncloaked, she is clearly rebellious, and I'm certain she helped the escaped girl. We found her near the factory."

Why was she still near the factory?

"Did you find the girl?"

"No." Hulk stepped back toward Eliza and towered over her like a cougar ready to strike. "And this treacherous vermin won't talk."

His hand came up, and I flew forward. "No!" My shoulder landed near his kidneys. "Don't touch her." I growled.

He staggered to the side and tripped, and we both landed on the platform.

"Don't ever touch her again."

My fist doubled, and I let it fly. A hand caught my shoulder and pulled me backward before I could land the blow.

"Enough." Jed spoke over me. He examined me, and a sheen passed over his eyes. But only for a moment. He straightened his posture and scowled. "She is Uncloaked. That is all the evidence we need. Her destination is a given."

"No." I scrambled to my feet and unzipped my coat. I couldn't slide my arms out of the sleeves fast enough to settle it over her shoulders. "She's under my protection now. I claim her."

Hulk pushed off the ground and stalked toward me. "That's not how that works, PK."

I glared at him and then looked to Jed. The skin around his eyes crinkled as lines in his forehead appeared. That was it. I'd found the loophole in their unwritten disgusting rule.

"You claim her..." Jed tipped his head to the side. "For how long?"

Seriously? My fist doubled again. "Forever," I spat.

His eyebrows quirked up. "Marriage to the Uncloaked...is that what you are proposing, Luther?"

I slid my arm around her shoulders and shifted so that I could see her eyes. She looked at me as though I'd just knelt on one knee and slipped a ring on her finger, and I knew her answer.

"Yes." My voice caught in my throat.

She laid her head against my shoulder, and I locked her in a possessive hold. "Eliza Knight is mine—you can't send her to a camp."

Hulk's laughter snaked over us and set a chill on my heart.

"No." He stepped forward, his swagger mocking the gravity of the moment. "That's not how this works. If she wants to stay in our society, she has to take the seal. No pledge, no citizenship. It's that simple."

My attention flew to Jed. He was the senior officer of the Jackals. The Party had endowed him with the power of decision. Eliza's life would be determined by his ruling.

He stared hard at me, his face masked in unreadable discipline, but the sheen passed again over his eyes. "Hulk is right. Eliza has to pledge if she is to stay."

Air couldn't get into my lungs. Violent shaking overtook my hands as I turned her to face me.

"Will you pledge?" There was a hint of regret in Jed's voice. Like he already knew the answer.

So did I.

Her gaze never left mine, and a single tear slipped onto her bruised cheek. Her lips trembled, but her quiet voice settled over the crowd with resolute conviction. "No."

My heart fell, landing on the jagged shards of our broken lives. I wrapped her in a fierce hold as the crowd shouted their outrage. Her face tucked into my shoulder, and a cry shuddered over me.

"I'm coming with you," I whispered.

"No." She leaned away and tipped her chin up until she found my mouth. Under the guise of a last kiss, she whispered against my mouth. "Save our people."

They tore us apart. Everything blurred as I fought against the hands that held me, roared against the Jackals who put her into a railcar, but I remembered her face with perfect clarity. She cried, and there had been fear in her eyes. But her faith never shifted. I finally understood the strength that had defined this girl whom I loved.

The girl who loved me.

CHAPTER TWENTY-THREE

"Name your charge, Lieutenant." The man spoke gravely, his thin dark mustache moving in cadence with his serious tone.

Hulk sent me a sideways glare as he stood at attention before the summoned Party official. Impartial. That was what Hulk had requested. An impartial judge who would decide my fate.

"Treason," he sneered. "Treason against the Party and against our new nation. Treason of the worst kind. Impersonating a loyal citizen. Espionage."

I faced forward, setting my face in a cold, blank stare. I refused to meet the official's inquisitive glance and wouldn't look over to Hulk. The guy was possessed. He had to be. How could a person be that mean? So calculative and cold and cruel.

He'd taken my Eliza and shipped her away. Emotion threatened to crack my hard exterior. I locked it down deep and maintained a face of stone.

"How do you plead?"

"Not guilty." Not because I hadn't done it, but because doing it didn't make me guilty. It was right. Eliza, my father, Evan, they'd all been right. Sometimes the right path was hard.

"What evidence do you bring against your brother, Lieutenant?"

A furnace inside of me exploded. *I am not his brother.* My jaw clamped tight.

"Eliza was his best friend. Can it be coincidence that his best friend—the girl he attempted to marry so that she wouldn't have to pay for her disloyalty—can it be possible that she just happened to know about a runaway prisoner? I doubt it."

"You didn't find Eliza with the prisoner." Jed stood as he spoke, his voice monotone. "You only found Eliza."

"I found her loopy in the woods near the factory. Close enough for implicating a Jackal, and no one else would betray us."

Loopy? Eliza had been loopy? Wha— *Oh no.* I had to concentrate on keeping my eyes from sliding shut and my knees from buckling. My heart twisted like a wrung-out rag. The bottle of persuasion. I'd stashed it in my pack, which I'd left in the mill. It was my fault. Eliza had been caught because I'd been careless.

Jed started speaking again. I listened while my world crumbled. "We can't put charges on a citizen and a Jackal just because you have assumptions, Hulk."

Just kill me. Please, just kill me.

"You are not fit to run our Den, Stevens!" Hulk turned to face Jed, his nostrils flaring. "You're only protecting him so that you can have a poster boy to lay before the Party."

207

Jed returned Hulk's venomous stare with a chilling calm. "I am protecting a citizen of the United States. You have taken the power granted you and twisted it into vengeance. This is not the face the Party needs. Remember, we still live in a democracy. Your crazed tactics will bring failure to our new order." He turned his attention back to the superior officer. "Luther was seen at the Commons the night the girl went missing. He was in his bunk after that, attended morning exercises the following day, and was accounted for in class. The lieutenant's claims can't be substantiated. It is my duty to present the facts."

The official bounced a look from Hulk to Jed, stroking his thin mustache. The judiciary room of the courthouse felt cold and ominous as his silence extended. "You." He pierced me with his beady eyes. "What do you have to say?"

I slid a look to him and met his stare, keeping all emotion off my face and out of my voice. "I just watched them ship the girl I love to a Reformation Camp." I swallowed, gaining control of the threatening quiver in my jaw.

"Don't you dare question my loyalty."

———

Like this book? Please add a short review on **Amazon** and let me know what you thought!

Want to know what comes next? Good news! **Tearing the Veil** is available **right here**, right now.

Keep reading for a sneak peek at the intense second install-ment of The Uncloaked Trilogy or find the full story at **Amazon**.

ABOUT THE AUTHOR

J. Rodes lives on the wide plains somewhere near the middle of Nowhere. A coffee addict, pickleball enthusiast, and storyteller, she also wears the hats of mom, teacher, and friend. Mostly, she loves Jesus and wants to see the kids she's honored to teach fall in love with Him too.

ACKNOWLEDGMENTS

This is the hard part. Not acknowledging those who make this dream happen, but narrowing the list of who will make print. Because it takes more than I ever dreamed. Here we go, though...

My family. You let me wander off into another world. Sometimes I come back uplifted. Other times, not so much. Yet you love me just the same. I am humbled by your joyous encouragement to my weirdness.

Sarah. I know you think I only need a broken record saying, "Keep writing, keep writing, keep writing..." But really, I need you. And Sondra. And Janet. And Lucy. You pick my head up off the floor when I face plant, tease a smile back to my lips, and remind me that this journey really isn't as lonely as I think.

Dori. Wow, I'm just grateful. Someday I might learn how to English, but until then, thanks for fixing my words, and being my cheerleader along the way.

And my Superman. I keep thinking you're going to get sick of me—my doubts, my featherbrained ways, and the fact that I still can't kitchen well. But you remain as constant as ever. The arms I fall into when I'm discouraged. The first one I call when I am bursting with excitement. My safe place. I love life with you.

Thank you all.

ALSO BY J. RODES

Tearing the Veil
The Uncloaked Book Two

Charging the Darkness
The Uncloaked Book Three

Emerald Illusion
(Coming 10/2018)

SNEAK PEEK OF TEARING THE VEIL

Braxton Luther

"We've got a stray spark on the run."

I wasn't sure who the voice belonged to as it came over my earpiece. All of us wore a vocal transmitter during a raid—it could have been any number of Jackals set on watch. My eyes burned as I stared into the fire we'd set. The roof was a black silhouette against the orange glow, and the walls groaned and snapped as the flames consumed them.

Standing across from my position near the front door, Hulk's anger contorted his already menacing face. "Where'd it come from?" he growled.

"West side," the voice responded.

Tristan's post. I forced an even breath and masked my hope with a scowl.

"I didn't see him," Tristan hissed over the intercom.

Hulk's contorted face smoldered as hot as the flames licking the house. "You'd better get 'em."

Heavy breathing rustled through the transmitter, and Tristan said, "I'm on it."

Run, kid. Although, if he got away, Tristan would end up with a trip to the locker. Maybe worse. At least I knew where he stood though.

"He's headed to the trees," the other voice tattled.

Was Hannah there waiting to help? Maybe Miranda?

Run! God, let him run faster.

I blinked against the searing heat in front of me—so I could remove the threatening tears burning against my eyes. I didn't know who lived in the house we'd torched, but I knew this family must have been faithful. Their home wouldn't be ablaze on this hot summer night if they hadn't been firmly against the Party. What had they done exactly? Arson was reserved for the people who posed real threats to the New Order. People of influence. They called them the Rebellion.

Or this kind of discipline came to the Cloaked. A shiver rippled down my arms despite the blaze. The Cloaked were the disloyal compliant, those who took the Party's seal only because doing so would keep their citizen status. Or, in my case—and Tristan's—those who became the mole in the system.

"He's quick, sir!" Tristan spoke again, his breathing still heavy.

Hulk's frame bulged with rage. "Meltzner, so help me, if you lose this kid, I will personally whip you with the claw. And trust me when I say your back will be nothing but ripped flesh when I'm done."

Pain locked hard in my stomach. That was not an empty threat.

An image of my father surfaced as I continued to stare into the flames. Had they stripped his flesh before they'd clamped him on the table? With vivid clarity, I could picture his tortured face: blue lips, bulging eyes, pale skin. Dead. Murdered by the hateful hands of the Party because he'd refused to take their seal. Because he was a rebel Uncloaked.

Labored panting filled my ears as I listened to the chase. The sound of snapping twigs and then a thud rumpled over the transmitter.

"What happened?" Hulk demanded.

"Badger hole," Tristan gasped. "I didn't see it…"

A child yelped in the background.

"Gotcha." The other voice hissed like a demon from the pit of hell. Probably not far from it. "He's a small boy—six or seven. I've got him."

I couldn't breathe as I glanced down to my shirt—the same shirt every Jackal wore. The mallet, the fist, and the creed were printed on the front. *Standing watch at home* branded the back. I hated every word. We were terrorists, not some kind of noble guard for the people.

Hulk crossed his muscle-bound arms over his bulldog chest. "Good. Bring him back." Flames gleamed in his eyes, chilling me through. The devil himself. "You're not in the clear, Meltzner. I'll still see you in the locker."

Invisible shackles tightened around my neck. I'd sold myself to the prince of hate. Now I was forced to watch the unfolding of his black heart. If only I'd listened before. To my father. To Eliza.

A crowd gathered on the sidewalk, which hit me as odd. That hadn't happened when the Jackals burned the Knights' home last year. No one had come then. No one had cared. Maybe this practice of torching the noncompliant was becoming a little too common to ignore.

My chest expanded as hope took a small breath. If people knew the truth...

"Can you tell us what happened here?" A woman, though speaking into her slender All-In-One (our government-issued everything device—communication, identification, currency—without it, no life) directed her question to Hulk.

Great. Exactly the wrong person for the truth.

"We got a call about some possible domestic violence." Hulk talked as if he were actually law enforcement. Not hardly. We were a bunch of puffed-up guys given way too much power. "It was already too late when we got here. But this wasn't domestic violence. This was a demonstration—a protest against our benevolent Party. This is why noncitizens are dangerous. Their nonconformist attitudes breed violence and destruction."

Liar. I ground my teeth, hardly managing to keep my loose cannon of a mouth glued shut.

"Were there any injuries?" the woman asked.

Hulk hung his head and shook it. "Unfortunately we were unable to rescue the family. The fire was already out of control by the time we made it to the scene. But one of our brave Jackals managed to rescue a small boy."

Heat surged white hot through my veins.

The woman tried to look concerned—just in case someone was running a video feed with their All-In-One, I was sure. "So sad. What will be done?"

"It is tragic." Hulk nodded, feigning empathy as if he were on a Broadway stage. "But thanks to our new system, we have good homes for orphans. He will be taken care of, educated, and given every advantage of a Sealed Citizen. If there's any bright spot in this horrific violence, that's it."

How could a guy who mercilessly hunted the Uncloaked

turn into this oversized man version of Mother Theresa without even a hint of regret? The things I saw as a Jackal would appall the average American. But they didn't know the truth. Apathy had given birth to a demented and ravenous son named Power, and Power had no moral compass at all.

I stepped away, balling my fists. Hot misery sunk into my body, pulling my shoulders low. I thought back to the night the Jackals had burned the Knights' house. Part of me had wished we had been lost to the flames.

I was living in the Den, yet I was among the hunted—the Cloaked. The cold, hungry breath of death brushed against my skin with every throb of my heart. But I had to survive. There were so many who needed help and so few who even knew to care.

I was there, in the Den, for such a time as this.

———

Hannah Knight

My hands trembled in the July heat. Dizzy waves crashed through my head, blurring the world around me and forcing me to stop. I slumped against a tree, fighting nausea and the blackness narrowing my vision. Food. If only Braxton could give us more this time.

No. If only we didn't live this life of the fearful hidden. Homeless, starving, sick, and worst of all, terrified. No one dreamed of this life. No one saw it coming. Now it was our everyday reality.

We grew what we could from the seeds that had been left in the barn, but only in little patches that we worked to make the plants blend with the rest of the forest. A few scattered potatoes here. A little grouping of onions there. A zucchini plant that hopefully mingled invisible with the wild gourds in narrow meadows. Nothing that would catch a hunter's attention.

One of the boys in our group had snared a rabbit the week before. One rabbit. For twenty starving people. It seemed more like torture than a blessing.

Maybe Reformation Camp wouldn't be that bad. At least they'd feed you. There would be a bed to sleep on rather than the damp earth, an actual toilet to use instead of a pit dug into the ground.

Or maybe Braxton's approach was the way to go. The Party had a group and a home for girls. The Pride. I'd turned fifteen last spring, so I was old enough to join.

Click, click...click.

Braxton. He and my sister had made up that call back when hide-and-seek was just a game.

Click, click...click.

I answered his call as the sun shifted, resting a ray of afternoon light on my cheeks. I ignored the warmth as it spread over my skin, concentrating instead on the irritation that spiraled in my stomach every time I used my sister's signal.

I loved her. Missed her. Envied her. That last part snarled around whatever it was that triggered things like irritation. Whenever someone spoke about Eliza, it was in hushed and hollowed tones. Because she was perfect. Smart. Strong. Always did what was right. And she—

Braxton's frame emerged from the barrier of trunks created by the dense forest. My breath snagged in my throat as he dropped to the ground near me. Did she feel like this with him?

He towered over me even when we were sitting, which made a girl feel like she could curl up next to him and (if he would wrap his arms around her) be completely safe. I looked into his eyes—light brown, the color of caramel, which I could stare at for hours. The dizziness returned, pouring over my body in tingling showers, and I slid my eyes closed, letting the image of his arms around me linger in my mind. I wasn't sure if it was the thought of food or that sweet fantasy that triggered the lightheadedness, but it also ignited irritation again.

I would never be in his arms.

Because of Eliza. Perfect, smart, good-to-the-bone Eliza. She always monopolized his attention.

"You okay?" His hand curved over my shoulder. Warm. Tingling, again.

"Yeah." I fluttered my eyes open and looked back at him. "Just hungry."

Eliza wasn't there. I moved to cover the hand that still rested on my shoulder. He slid it away from my touch but curved his arm around me to give me a side big-brother kind of hug before he shifted to settle his backpack between us.

A chill replaced my lightheaded hope. It wasn't fair. He'd never notice me, even if we knew for a fact Eliza was dead. Not that I wanted her to be dead. That would be really, really sad. Honest. But, I was there, and he was hurting... Even still, he only ever saw me as her little sister. Not even as her interesting little sister—which I was. The only thing I had on my saintly sis was a personality. Eliza was utterly predictable. I, on the other hand, was more like Braxton...which was way more exciting.

I shook my head, heat flooding my face. Only when I was with Braxton did I think things like that. I looked to my knees as guilt poured through my body. Eliza had been shipped off to some cruel, fix-your-attitude-or-die camp, and here I sat beside her *best friend* (anyone with eyes knew they were definitely way more than friends), thinking about how I was better for him than she was.

"Here." He brushed my elbow with his knuckles and then handed me the bagel in his hand. "You eat all of this. You look smaller than the last time I saw you."

He noticed my size? I bit my lip, restricting a smile. "Thanks."

He nodded, his beautiful eyes serious, and then looked away at the forest, focusing on nothing. The threat of a smile on my lips died. He'd noticed that I was starving. That was all. I tore a bit off the dry bagel and shoved it into my mouth. As soon as it hit my taste buds, my stomach demanded more. Braxton's attention fell back on me, and I covered my growling belly with my free hand.

"Sorry," I said.

His mouth tilted in a sad smile. "No, I'm sorry." He ran a hand over his head and looked away again. "I'm sorry I can't get you guys more."

The ink near his shirt collar caught my attention, and I fingered my own neck. Girls in the Pride didn't starve. They weren't objects of charitable obligation. They were brave, intelligent, and admired. They didn't cower in the forest, forever afraid.

Bet they had their pick of the Jackals.

I shoved another bite of bagel into my mouth, forcing myself to chew completely before swallowing. Braxton sat wordless, still staring off into nothing—probably wishing he was sitting here with Eliza instead of with me.

Well, fine. I wasn't my sister. Might as well just settle that. I wasn't Eliza. I didn't do the things Eliza would do.

But I was willing to do what she refused.

I settled my gaze on his profile. Strong, set jawline, straight nose, distracting lips... My heart rate jumped. If he could only see me.

"I could help you," I said.

Braxton's head whipped back to me, the intensity of his eyes setting off an excited flutter in my stomach.

"What are you talking about?" His dark tone was like a dart pinning that foolish flutter, striking it dead.

I poked my shoulders straight. "What you did." I lifted my chin. "I could get sealed. I'm old enough to join the Pride."

His gaze turned into a glare. "No."

"What?"

"No."

I scowled. "You practically begged Eliza—"

He launched to his feet. "I was wrong." He spun to face me, anger sizzling in his look. "I was dead wrong, and Eliza paid—" His voice cracked, and he looked away. Both of his hands covered his head. After two long breaths, he looked back at me. "Don't ever say that again." His hand braced against the tree I leaned on as he glowered over me. "Don't even think it. Got it, Hannah?"

End of discussion. He actually scared me a little with that demanding, intense stare. I felt like a dumb little girl. So much for hoping he'd be impressed. Why did Eliza always have to be right? Why did Braxton have to...

I wasn't going there. Sighing, I forced my mind down another path.

"We're leaving soon." I tried to ignore that stupid, small feeling he'd provoked. I wasn't a little kid, and Braxton didn't keep charge over me. "The scout contacted Dad. The first group made it to the Refuge. We'll leave before fall."

"Good." Braxton pushed away from the tree and sat beside me again. "You'll be safe there."

"You think."

"Don't do that." A firm frown punctuated his command. "Cynicism won't do you any favors. Choose to hope."

I snorted. "This from Patrick Luther's rebel son."

One eyebrow on his face arched. "That's right. So I would know, wouldn't I?"

My cheeks grew hot, and I swallowed. "Sorry," I mumbled, looking at my feet. I swallowed again and drew a full breath. "You should come with us." I chanced a sideways look, though I didn't raise my head.

"I can't," he said.

Two words, but they said a hundred other things. He wouldn't—refused even to discuss it. He would never stop looking for Eliza. Wouldn't forgive himself for how everything turned out. Couldn't come to terms with all that had happened the year before.

"You really loved her, didn't you?" I whispered, staring at what was left of the bagel he'd given me. I could feel his gaze on me but couldn't make myself look. Didn't want to see his answer.

"I'll always love your sister."

Yeah, I knew that. The knot in my chest pulled tighter. Next to my sister, I'd never measure up.

———

Braxton

Why would she even think about the Pride? Didn't she understand that I lived in a nightmare? How could two sisters be so completely different anyway?

Hannah was headed for trouble. She needed to leave. Soon. Now.

But for the moment, I had to protect her. I owed Eliza at least that much. No, I owed her so much more than she understood, than anyone understood, and the guilt sat like a slow burn in my stomach every single day.

God, is she still alive? She had to be alive. She still called to me in my dreams.

My attention fell back to Hannah, who sat stiff by my side. The girl was spinning in her head like a tire on a bicycle, and because she was way too much like me, I could guess what she was thinking.

"It isn't better out there." I tipped her chin so I could see her eyes—something I usually tried to avoid. They looked like Eliza's, and I hated the ache that pressed into my chest. But I needed to make sure she was listening. "You've got to believe me on this. It's not what you think. Stay with your family. Go to the Refuge."

She stared back at me, but not like Eliza would have. Eliza would listen—hear what I was saying and process it intelligently, which was why she could always come up with a logical answer to my dumb schemes. Hannah...well, she processed with emotion, just like me. There was no reasoning with emotion.

I sighed and began transferring the food I'd squirreled away from the Den to her burlap sack. "You'd better get going. Remember, never the same place two times in a row, okay?"

Still stiff, she stood and, with a cool nod, took the sack. Not listening. Not good.

"Hannah, wait." I couldn't let this happen. "I need to

speak with your dad. Tell him I asked for him to meet me next time. Okay?"

She dipped one curt nod.

Great.

"I really need to talk to him...alone," I said, knowing that last part was going to spark her defiance.

An icy stare was her only response. So not like Eliza.

I pushed my fingers through my hair, stuffing a growl down into my chest. "Do you even know why you're mad?"

She spun on her worn-out tennis shoe, and I watched her shoulders, jammed straight and rebellious, as she wove through the trees.

Fine. Just as long as she was stomping back to the cellar. She had no business thinking about the Pride.

CONTINUE THE CHALLENGE NOW!

Available in digital, print, and audio formats at **Amazon.**

Made in the USA
Middletown, DE
17 January 2019